WASTED

NICOLA MORGAN

**WALKER
BOOKS**

First published 2010 by Walker Books Ltd
87 Vauxhall Walk, London SE11 5HJ

4 6 8 10 9 7 5

Text © 2010 Nicola Morgan

The right of Nicola Morgan to be identified as author of this work
has been asserted by her in accordance with the
Copyright, Designs and Patents Act 1988

This book has been typeset in Bembo, Justlefthand and Carnival

Printed and bound in Great Britain by Clays Ltd, St Ives plc

British Library Cataloguing in Publication Data:
a catalogue record for this book is available from the British Library

ISBN 978-1-4063-2195-1

www.walker.co.uk

WASTED

IMAGINE THE SCENE:

Jack and Jess in a club, wrapped up in each other. An enemy, Kelly, waits her moment to spike Jess's drink. Another girl is outside, trying to get past the bouncer, who may or may not let her in.

He might be distracted or annoyed – such small things can make all the difference. If she gets in, she'll distract Jess's friends and they won't see the drink being spiked. If she doesn't get in, Jess's friends will see what happens and save her. The reader sees both scenes, until a coin is tossed and one possibility vanishes. In *Wasted*, the reader witnesses alternative results unfold and disappear, as the lives of Jack and Jess spin out of control. Finally, it is you who must take the risk and toss a coin to determine the ending. Their lives are in your hands.

Wasted is a startling story of danger, passion and chance by Nicola Morgan, the award-winning author of *Fleshmarket* and *Deathwatch*.

You can find out more about Nicola and her books at:
www.nicolamorgan.co.uk

Books by the same author

Chicken Friend
Deathwatch
Fleshmarket
The Highwayman's Footsteps
The Highwayman's Curse
Mondays Are Red
The Passionflower Massacre
Sleepwalking

Blame My Brain
Know Your Brain
The Leaving Home Survival Guide

This one's for Harry, Hannah and Rebecca,
with all my love

CHAPTER 1
WAITING

JESS is spinning a coin. Not actually playing Jack's Game yet, because if you're going to play you have to be very sure. Heads or tails, win or lose, life or death: playing the game changes things and you can't escape its rules.

She thinks – because she has thought about this quite a lot in the last day and a bit – that if there's a God, He must play Jack's Game. There's not really any other explanation she can think of.

Jess is sitting in a horrible waiting room the colour of old white socks. Waiting. The waiting is awful. It numbs her. Though perhaps waiting for ever would be better than knowing. She wants her guitar, but it wouldn't exactly be appropriate. You can't sing in a place like this.

On the floor is a grubby doll with no clothes and one leg. It lies there with blue eyes open. It looks shocked, or dead. There is pen scribbled on its stomach and someone has tried to cut its hair. Jess remembers doing that to a doll once, convinced that it would grow again.

Jess is seventeen years old. Her dad's a genetic scientist, apparently. Her mum's an alcoholic. If you tossed a coin, chances are she could take after either or both of them. Trouble is, her dad lives 4,000 miles away and her mum lives next door to her bedroom. This probably alters her chances.

A flash of anger crosses Jess's mind. She thinks that if she saw the Kelly Gang now she'd want to… But no, best not to think like that. Jess is not prone to violent thoughts. But she is in a state of shock, and strange feelings are stirring. She tries to think about anything else.

The bracelet she's wearing. A birthday present from her best friend, Chloe. That was a good day: her mum remembered to rustle up a cake – all the way from Mrs Beaton's Tea Shoppe – and they ate it on the beach, digging their bare heels into the shingle and breathing the seashell air. Her dad phoned and sent the usual money.

But Jess is scared and it's hard to keep her mind on such things as cake, though she must try. So: it was a fantastic cake; she and her mum used their fingers to scrape the chocolate icing off the wrapping; they have the best cakes in Mrs Beaton's Tea Shoppe.

If she saw the Kelly Gang now she'd want to kill them. To be honest. Not very nice, but then why should Jess feel *nice*?

Keep spinning the coin, Jess. It will help. Focus on that coin. Don't drop it. That's better.

Jess is trying to make a decision. Does she dare play the game? The sensible part of her knows she shouldn't. After all, she managed to stop Jack taking it so seriously. But Jack's Game *is* serious, and perhaps it's all she can do now. Maybe all the spirits and gods and everything else that has a say in the world watch when you play Jack's Game. Maybe that's what gives it its power. It's like ancient magic, but with science. According to Jack. Now she is confused and alone and needing him to take the decision away, but when she thinks back to the newspaper stories on his bedroom wall, she knows what he would do. She just can't decide whether he's right.

Jess is more than confused and alone. She is barely holding herself together. If she breathes too hard she may shatter into a million pieces.

She glances at the clock. Still spinning the coin. With remarkable skill, considering that she's only been practising for two weeks. It almost ripples across her fingers, weaving in and out, a life of its own. Left hand as good as the right. That'll be the piano-playing, and guitar. Someone comes through the door. A woman. Her eyes are puffy. She grips the hand of a bewildered child with chocolate on its face. Jess doesn't want to look at her, but she's drawn by her grief. The woman picks up the dead doll and gives it to the child, who grins and grabs it by its remaining leg. Jess thinks that if she was the child's mother she'd make her daughter clean and dress it and learn how to love it in more ways than just holding on. The door clunks shut and the air settles again.

Jess rummages in her bag and gets out her iPod, plugs her ear-things in and retreats into her music. Their music. The colours wash over her and her senses merge. She closes her eyes, keeps the outside out: the Kelly Gang, the smell, the being really scared. Yesterday. Saturday. Everything. Her mum should be here. Her dad. Someone. A girl shouldn't be in such a place on her own. But then Jess didn't tell anyone she was coming so early, so you can hardly blame them.

She opens her eyes suddenly, rips out the ear-things. *Breathe slowly, Jess. Almost lost it there. Maybe music is not such a good idea right now, or at least not this particular song. Maybe you should read a magazine. Something shallow, something that won't slice its way deeper than skin.*

Actually, apart from the old sock colour, the room's not that bad. Soft chairs. Tea and coffee. Free. Plants. A fish tank. They've made an effort, just to stop you thinking. Box of tissues. Cushions. You can't hear sounds from outside, except when the door opens, though there's a buzzing of air-con. It's designed to help you forget where you are. So there's a magazine on sailing and one on houses. And some children's books and toys. She picks up a board book for babies or toddlers or whatever and looks at pictures of diggers and cranes and just does not allow herself to think of what's past that door and what will happen when she is told to walk through it.

Probably she will spin the coin soon and play Jack's Game. After all, a fifty-fifty chance is not that bad. The truth could be a whole lot worse.

CHAPTER 2
POSSIBLY A DEAD BODY

A dead body is a strange thing the first time you see one. It depends how death has struck, of course. From inside or from out. With fire or water or suffocation, disease, poison, any number of things. The body could be broken or whole. If you see it in a morgue they will have used a sheet to cover the broken bits. If possible. Unless it has been damaged by flames, a white person's body is generally a sort of waxy grey in death. Like a dirty candle that's too wet to light.

A body that has been washed up from the sea is not the best. This one has already drunk some salty water and is swollen. You don't really want to look at it too closely. It is greyer than a human should be, fish-like and damp.

Jess has never liked the word "damp". Nothing damp is attractive.

But wait: this dead body thing has not happened yet. It is the future and therefore may turn out differently.

It is one possibility of many. It depends what leads to it. Things need to happen and before that, others.

If we roll the clock back to a time before the dead-body scene, we see Jess somewhere else entirely. Nowhere near this beach beyond the town lights, not running screaming along the shingle towards the human heap that sprawls in the froth, her clothes sticky with sweat and sea-spray and vodka, and grimy with wood smoke.

We see her spinning through the excitement of the leavers' prom. She is wrapped up in heat and laughter, the heady feeling when she sang her last long note and the band stopped playing and the cheers rose. Strange hot tears. She will soon head into the night with Jack for the beach party. She has no idea that everything is about to spiral out of control. If it was ever in control.

When it is all over, will she remember the smell of Jack when she buried her face in his neck? How it made her feel faint?

Our story moves too fast. We should roll back to the beginning; except that there never is a beginning. Everything comes from something else. Nothing just happens out of the so-called blue.

For the sake of argument, we will take up the tangled chain of events two weeks ago, two weeks before the possible dead body lies on the beach, two weeks before Jess is in that old-sock waiting room. Maybe, even, she won't get there. It could all turn out quite differently. Kelly…

Jess and Jack and their friends are hurtling towards what they call freedom. And more choices than they know what to do with.

CHAPTER 3
WHEN JACK MET JESS

THE moment when Jack hears Jess sing so nearly doesn't happen.

Jess doesn't know she's left the door of the music room slightly open. It shouldn't have been possible, not in the new soundproofed studio with its heavy sprung doors, but it was not exactly unknown for something not to work properly in this school. If the door had been firmly closed, Jess's voice would have been confined in the room, Jack would have hurried past and Jess would have stayed safely out of his dangerous life.

If Jess hadn't received a text from Chloe as she was entering the room, she might have taken more care closing the door. Also, there was a brown banana skin on the floor, its smell nastying the warm air, so she'd focused on kicking that aside rather than whether the door was closed.

Besides, she's been in that studio plenty of times before and the door has always shut without effort. On this occasion, however, perhaps a few extra specks of dust settling on the hinge on a humid day have created just enough tension for the springs to stick. It could have happened the day before, or the day after. Even the cleverest scientist or machine in the world could not have predicted when that door would stick.

None of this would have mattered if Jack hadn't walked past the door when he did. After all, he shouldn't have been there. Didn't even go to Northseas High School. He used to – he'd left to go to a nearby sixth-form college two years ago, the same time Jess had arrived in the area and started at Northseas, so he'd never met her.

So, why is he there? Well, Jack has a band and they have been signed up to play at the leavers' prom at Northseas. Jack is supposed to be meeting the deputy head to sort out details. He's signed into reception as a visitor, got his visitor's ID badge thing, smiled at the receptionist as he agreed that yes, he did still know the way. The receptionist had always liked Jack. A nice boy, she thought, though his hairstyle had now become rather unusual. If she'd been his mother she'd have made him get it *sorted*, but she suspected that Jack thought that sorted was exactly what it already was. Besides, as everyone knew, he didn't have a mother.

There are two routes Jack could have taken to the deputy head's office: the shorter way past the library or the longer way through the music department. He has chosen the longer way, even though he is running late. Why?

You might think: well, he is a musician, drawn to the music department. But this is Jack, this is school, so no, the school music department has no special magnetism for him.

It was Kelly Jones. Walking along the corridor towards him, accompanied by Samantha. They didn't see him, but they would have if he'd continued that way. There are many unpleasant bits of Northseas High and Kelly and Samantha are extremely prominent on the list of them. There's a specific reason for Jack wanting to avoid Kelly, but we won't go into that now. It's complicated. And uncomfortable to remember. Though Jack does not yet know how important it will become.

For now, he has more pressing stuff on his mind than Kelly. Problems in his band: Janey, the singer, has walked out. At any other time this wouldn't have mattered. She'd been a pain in the neck anyway, a prima donna with a serious attitude problem, and late for practice most times. Trouble is, it's only two weeks before the event and Jack's band has no singer. Jack has decided not to tell the deputy head, Mrs Willow. He'll find a singer somewhere. The rest of the band said he should tell Willow, but he disagreed. And sometimes there's something about Jack that makes it hard to argue with him. So, eventually, they let him decide it by tossing a coin. *Heads, we tell her; tails, we don't and something will turn up*. And the coin had fallen tails up. Which is enough for Jack, whose life has in the past been ruled by luck so horrible that he reckons he's used up all the bad fortune he is ever going to have.

Jack knows – believes, trusts, assumes, in a way that looks perhaps like arrogance, endearing optimism or foolish naïveté – that something will turn up. It always seems to if you look for it enough and make the right sacrifices to luck. Lucky Jack, you might say. Though someone whose mother has died twice is hardly lucky.

Anyway, it doesn't matter whether you call it luck or something else: Jack is walking along the corridor as Jess begins to sing. It is an amazing voice, deep, rich, warm. Very sexy. He doesn't know the song but he wants to.

He stops and listens. Surely this must be a recording. It cannot be real. Not in a school.

Jess often comes here now. Exams have finished for her, so she doesn't need to come for classes, but the equipment is here and perhaps she's clinging to something familiar while she gets used to the strange idea of school being nearly over. A few of her friends are still immersed in exams; the others, like Chloe, have disappeared on weird leavers' courses designed to prepare them for the "real" world and keep them out of trouble.

But, for Jess, music is not about exams or teachers. It is all of her, or all she wants to think about. She's written a new song and so she keeps coming to the school's state-of-the-art recording studio, putting on the headphones and losing herself as she writes it down, makes it just right, getting used to using a mic. The guitar chords are tricky, but she has them almost perfect now and she can let herself go, not needing to think too much about the fingering. She closes her eyes. This is what it would be like to be professional, singing for a career. A swooping feeling clutches at her stomach every time she dreams it.

It's only when she's actually singing that Jess can believe this dream. The rest of the time, there seem to be way too many obstacles. Decisions. Should she have applied to music college after all? She'd wanted to, and her teachers had encouraged her but money wasn't easy and her mum had played that card hard – probably because college meant Jess going away. And Jess knew what her mother felt about that. So she didn't apply and then she got caught up in exams anyway. She kind of thought that something would turn up, or she'd maybe take a year out, earn some money, go travelling and then think about it again.

The nagging fear of leaving school with no plans was something she brushed away at first – it seemed like another world. But now it doesn't and the closer it comes, the more Jess is churned by anxiety. Sometimes it makes her dizzy to think about it, especially when she sees her friends get their plans sorted out.

But she feels excitement too. For the freedom. Away from school and exams and rules and some people she's spent too long looking at every day. Away from home, too, though *that* isn't going to be simple. Nothing that involved her mother ever was. Not that she actually wants to think about her mum being on her own. It's an issue. But, much as she loves her mum, it is not her job to look after her. It should be more her dad's responsibility. Yeah, right: responsibility. On the other hand, her dad doesn't know about the drinking. Jess hasn't told him. She wants to protect her mum, and she knows what he'd say.

Confusing, this. All of it. She is entangled.

Jess's mum, Sylvia, is what you'd call "needy". Arty, flighty, moody, fragile. She has a vague rabbit look of fear in her eyes when they discuss Jess's future. She'll start fiddling with her cigarette lighter. And she drinks a lot more than she used to. Or maybe she always used to and Jess didn't notice before, because Sylvia used to be better at hiding it. But probably it has crept up on Sylvia as gradually as it has dawned on Jess. Neither really wants to face it. Jess wants to think she's wrong, or that it will solve itself.

When she's singing, she can forget about all that.

A sound makes Jess jump. She opens her eyes, stops singing halfway through a word, rips the earphones off and glares at the face at the door. A boy is there, looking at her. The door is ajar and he is half inside the room, hair hanging over one eye, mouth open slightly. He has a large mouth. And not in a bad way.

"Hi," he says. "Look, I'm in a hurry and I just need you to say yes."

"Who are you?"

"You won't regret it."

"I'm regretting it already. What do you want? And it's probably no, whatever it is. And who are you?"

"I need you."

She rolls her eyes, flicks the page of her music. But she can't help a tiny smile inside. She's only human.

"No," he holds up his hands, "not in that way. This is not a corny chat-up scenario. I need you in my band. Please say you're not in a band already." His skin is smooth, the jaw strong, that smile huge.

"I don't know anything about you, or your band. No, I'm not. And I don't know if…"

"Just say yes. Please. I'm desperate. You'll save me. And you should be in a band. You should be in the best band. Mine."

"What's the band?" Jess already knows she is going to say yes, but she will spin it out a bit.

"Schrödinger's Cats. We're…"

"You're playing at the prom!"

"Not without a singer. That's why I need you. We lost our singer and I'm just going for a meeting with Willow and I'd really like not to have to lie to her. Please. You don't want me to lie, do you?"

She can only see one of his eyes because the other one is hidden by a flop of hair, but the one she can see is warm and blue, the lashes dark. Assuming that the other one matches, they are great eyes. Great hair too, obviously a lot of effort going on there. Sort of swooping bits at different angles. Like several ski jumps designed by someone with a sense of humour and serious engineering skills. Some streaks that might be the sun or they might not. Maybe he is one of the surfing types that hang out at the beach and get themselves looking all Australian. Though his skin looks a bit pale for that.

"But it's only two weeks away. How can I learn the songs?"

"I'll teach you. You can do it. You have the most brilliant voice. It's perfect! We need you badly. You have to say yes. How can you not?" His words are falling over themselves.

She hesitates. Deliberately. Looks away from him, to hide her excitement. "Well, OK, but I can't promise I'll be able to learn everything."

"Yesss!" And now he is smiling and his smile is... "Look, can I call you later and can you be free this evening? Here, write your number on this. And what's your name?"

"Jess. And yes to the other things." She writes her number on the scrap of paper he rips from a pile on the table. She feels his eyes on her as she writes. It's not an unpleasant feeling.

"Thanks, Jess! I'll call you later."

"What's your name?" But he has gone.

Jess is surprised to find her heart beating hard, her body hot and a smile on her face that will not go away. She closes the door, firmly, and tries to get back to the song she was singing, but it doesn't work. She's heard that Schrödinger's Cats are good, even though they are just local. And even though they've got a weird name that sounds a bit pretentious. All at the sixth-form college, she's heard. She almost went to a gig once but the bouncers had other ideas and her fake ID wasn't good enough.

Her friends will be amazed when they find she is singing with the band that is playing at the prom.

Jack hurries through the school, along the familiar crisp-strewn corridors with their smell of disinfected toilets. He had known something would turn up and it has. This girl, Jess, that voice, the kind of Mediterranean hair, caramel skin and huge dark eyes, everything. She must be part Greek or Italian or something. He grins and is still grinning when he knocks on the door of Mrs Willow's office.

He is about ten minutes late but her annoyance soon melts in the face of his charm. Jack has always got away with things. It's difficult for an adult to believe that a boy with such a smile, such artistically arranged hair and two dead mothers to his name could mean any harm.

And he doesn't. Mean any harm. But Jack is dangerous to know. He killed his first mother during his own birth, just by being born – a cerebral haemorrhage, horribly rare, and everything happened too quickly for them to save her. Chance in a million, the doctors said, shaking their heads, as his father held this wrinkled scrap of baby in his hands and wondered how he would get through the next few minutes, days, weeks. Obviously, Jack doesn't remember that mother. His father married again when Jack was two years old. He does remember this new mother. She lasted three years, died when he was five, on his first day at school, and he was there that time too. She'd been playing football with him. In the kitchen. It was the sort of thing she did. Spontaneous, lived for fun, his dad said to him in later years. Didn't do things the normal adult way. She loved mess and breaking rules and wearing the wrong clothes for the occasion – not that he remembers that, but his dad said.

His dad is the sensible, organized one, the one who thinks things should be done in their proper places, or chaos ensues. Trouble is, that afternoon his dad wasn't there, otherwise the dishwasher would not have been open, the cutlery rack full, sharp knives pointing upwards, while his wife and young son were playing football in the kitchen. They should have been tackling Jack's brand-new reading book, but while Jack was getting the book out of his school-bag, he had dropped the football he was trying to carry at the same time. And when the ball had rolled towards her, it had been too tempting to ignore, so she'd made as if to dribble it; which had been too tempting for him to ignore, so he'd responded by kicking a beaut of a shot straight past her to the imaginary goal in the corner. It was a game they'd often played. Nothing had gone wrong before. Apart from a broken plate once, but what's a broken plate when you're having fun?

"Brilliant!" she had shouted, a split second before losing her balance and falling backwards onto a long kitchen knife sticking up in the dishwasher rack.

He remembers that. He remembers laughing because

she had looked so funny falling backwards, her face split open in wide-eyed surprise as she tried to grab something on her way down. Her shoes had made a funny squeak on the floor, he remembers, like a squashed mouse. Not that a squashed mouse is funny.

Then he'd stopped laughing. "Mummy! Get up! Get up!" But she didn't get up. She didn't move at all, apart from a strange juddering that he did not understand, until suddenly her body relaxed and he ran out of the kitchen. He could hear someone screaming and years later he realized that it must have been him, as there was no one else in the house.

Now "mother deceased" is in his school file. "Mothers deceased" might have been more accurate. So everyone knows that he is the boy whose second mother died on his first day at school, though often they forget, because he seems so OK. After all, it was many years ago now. There have been a couple of "aunts" and a couple of "friends" and Jack's life does not lack a feminine touch. Social services were a nuisance at first, but they have long since given up, once they realized that Jack's father could manage perfectly well. Jack's father is not going to risk trying to provide a mother for his son again.

The result of this is that Jack has become dangerous. His first mother had been a mountaineer – she'd given up when she was pregnant with Jack and had planned not to go back to it. Too dangerous, she'd said, too dangerous for a mother. Bit ironic, that, thinks Jack when his dad tells him, much later, considering that becoming a mother was what killed her. His second one had been a stunt double in her younger years and had never had a serious injury. Then she plays football with a small boy in an ordinary semi-detached house in an ordinary town in England and look what happens.

Stuff happens, is what, thinks Jack. There's no better explanation for half of it so people call it chance, though he calls it luck because he doesn't believe in chance. Jack worships luck. He believes that you make your own. He has thought it through, with his philosophy course feeding his interest, and soon he will probably tell Jess about it because they will have many conversations over the next two weeks. That's certain. You can see it in their eyes. One thing following from another.

Meanwhile, Jack has finished his meeting with Mrs Willow, and Mrs Willow is convinced that Jack has everything under control with his band. She trusts him, nice boy that he is, with that warmth in his eyes – or the one that she can see.

And Jess is almost home now, carrying her music-case as well as a bag of food that she's picked up from the supermarket, because her mum won't have. The air is heavy and damp with heat and the seaweed smell of a summer tide. A low sun glares in her eyes and her back feels sticky against her shirt. She is looking forward to a shower, changing, kicking off her shoes, something cold to drink, putting some music on. She's looking forward to telling her mum that she's in a band – in fact, joining a band had originally been a suggestion of her mum's, instead of the more expensive route of music college. Though Sylvia may change her mind about that when she thinks about it more carefully.

Jess hums her new song as she arrives at the gate.

Her steps become a little slower as she walks up the garden path. Home is sometimes a difficult place to be, even though it can be the best place too, and she can't be sure what mood her mum will be in. It will partly depend whether she's sold a painting, which is what she was hoping for that day. It's been a long time since she has sold one and on the one hand it's about time her luck changed; on the other hand, maybe she's lost her creativity. That's what Sylvia said, one evening recently, in a weepy session which began something like "What's the point of any of it?" and finished with "What's the point of any of it?" and another glass of wine downed quickly.

But most of all, Jess is looking forward to the moment when Jack will phone. Though she doesn't know his name yet. Which makes her wonder if he is real.

Spike jumps off the top of the wheelie bin where he has been sunbathing and comes to rub his body against her leg. She bends down and strokes his hot black back.

Sweet peas and deep raspberry pink roses clamber up some twisty sticks in pots and their smell is rich and fresh. It makes her want to breathe deeply. If you could trap moments and memories in a jar to taste later, this would be one: before arriving home, before anything, waiting, hoping, wishing, an unspoilt feeling. The present. Jess desires the future, but she is sometimes afraid of it. It is tangled with uncertainty. At least the present is something she knows. She is torn.

Spike pushes ahead of her as she opens the door.

CHAPTER 4
WHAT THE HOUSE SEES

THE house is silent and airless. It has the stillness of a house that has fallen asleep through boredom while its occupants have been away. It smells of the morning's toast. The post – nothing interesting – lies on the doormat. Breakfast dishes sit unwashed in the kitchen. The light on the answerphone is winking, and Jess plays the single message while she runs water and quickly does the dishes.

It's her mum. The voice is all high and sing-songy. So, it's been a good day. "Hi, darling. Um, you're obviously out – sorry, I can't remember if you said you had something on. I forgot to leave you a note. Hey – I called in at the gallery and guess what! They sold something! Yay! I'll be back about six but then I'm going out with Julia, so you can get your own tea. And don't forget to feed Spike!"

No, Jess will not forget to feed Spike. Jess never forgets to feed Spike. And buy the milk and bread and whatever they need. Though what will happen to Spike and the bread and the milk and life's other essentials when she's left home, who knows? And one day she *will* leave home, in the natural course of events. But Sylvia can't talk about that, won't think about it. And Jess is too afraid to push her. Sylvia has been left once, though it's about seven years ago now, and she can't bear to think about being left again. So she doesn't. After all, she could be knocked over by a bus before then. Or slip on a banana skin. Or any of the other things that never happen. Like lightning striking twice. Something will turn up. Jess will just move down the road, maybe, which won't really count as leaving. Sylvia can still call on her when she wants.

If there was a prize for burying one's head in the sand, Sylvia would win it. The International Ostrich Prize for running from reality.

Jess feeds Spike and tidies the kitchen quickly. She runs the tap till it is as cold as it will get, pours some into a glass with juice, chucks in some ice, cuts a piece of cheese and twists off some grapes. Some of those flatbreads with seeds. A chocolate biscuit. She'll make herself a meal later. Checks that there's some pasta sauce and salad things. Her phone is sitting on the kitchen side. She keeps looking at it. Sure enough, it rings. And it is an unknown number, which probably means...

"Hi, it's Jack."

"Hi." She opens the door to the garden and goes outside with her snack on a plate balanced in the crook of her arm, puts it on a rickety table and sits on the old swing hanging from an apple tree heavy with unripe fruit. Nearly six o'clock but the sun is still warm. It slants through the trees and toasts her skin. He's easy to talk to and the words just glide from them both. There's excitement in his voice, and she feels something spring alive inside her. She tells him a bit about herself, the songs she writes. They discover that neither of them has brothers and sisters.

"Just me and my mum. And cat," she says. "My dad lives in the States. Chicago."

"Just me and my dad," he says.

"Your mum?" she asks. His answer comes so easily that she doesn't even regret asking.

"She died. Ages ago."

"Sorry."

"Yeah, thanks. It's OK. It was a long time ago."

"So, when am I going to start learning these songs?"

They arrange that she'll go to his house that evening. It's fifteen minutes' walk away and he will meet her halfway so she doesn't get lost.

How charming. But then Jack is. It's why adults like him. Despite the hair that swoops across his face and sticks out in strange shapes that defy gravity. Jess likes him for other reasons, and *charming* is not something she would have consciously valued. She likes him for his eyes and smile and because he likes her and because electricity travels across the space between them. It's not complicated.

She does not know that he's dangerous. He doesn't look dangerous. But she wouldn't mind if he was. It's a chance she would definitely take.

She hears her mum come into the house. "Gotta go. See you seven-thirty."

Jess goes back inside. She squints after the brightness of the garden. And shivers.

"Hi, Mum. Great news about the painting!"

"Oh, Jess, it's fantastic!" Sylvia spins in a dance around the hall, scoops up Spike from a chair and buries her face in his fur. Spike is not entirely happy about this and wriggles away. Sylvia is wearing a floral drifty dress with thin straps. Her shoulders are tanned. Her eye make-up has slid into the cracks around her eyes. She kicks her feet from little sandals and bends down to rub a reddened toe. Jess's mum is not used to wearing shoes. In her studio, shared with a co-operative of artists, she doesn't wear any, though she'll wear huge socks when it's cold. And often she works outside, barefoot in the summer, maybe on the beach where she paints her favourite semi-abstract seascapes, trying to catch the light and the breeze and the smell of salt. Jess's mum is creative and does things in creative ways that do not fit in boxes. It's much safer in a box, but there are no rainbows.

Jess follows her into the kitchen and watches her pour a glass of chilled wine and drink a few fast sips before opening the fridge again to hunt for some food. Jess thinks she could do with a wash first – there is a cumin-seed smell of body odour. Her mum should not let herself go. But the thing is: she never actually had hold of herself in the first place.

Sylvia is plastering ripe Gorgonzola on an oatcake. Her blonde hair is long and wavy. Jess's is dark and wavy, though not as dark as her father's. Jess is a mixture of her mum's Scandinavian paleness and her father's Italian dark olive. Her own skin is a natural honey colour, as though permanently suntanned, but it annoys her because it seems to say something about who she is, and it shouldn't. Half her father and half her mother, when she doesn't feel like either of them. It speaks of their fractured family. Three separate people, with Jess in the middle, the magnet that draws them together and forces them apart.

"I'm celebrating with Julia tonight," her mum says. "We're going to that new restaurant and then maybe somewhere after that. Or we might both come back here."

"I'm going out too," says Jess.

"That's nice."

"Do you want to know where I'm going?"

"Sorry, where are you going?" Sylvia isn't even looking at her daughter. She's raiding the fridge. "Do we have any chutney? I've got a craving for chutney."

Sylvia, the mother, should know if they have any chutney. It is not Jess's responsibility to know if there's any chutney in the house, since she doesn't eat it.

"It's in the door of the fridge, Mum. I'm going to

meet someone who has a band. He wants me to be the singer."

"Are you sure?" What sort of question is that? What does Sylvia mean? Does she not trust her daughter to know?

"Yes, I'm sure. We're going to be playing at the leavers' prom."

"That'll be fun. Did you get some more bread?" Sylvia is looking in the bread bin.

"Yes, here – I haven't put it in the bread bin yet."

"Thanks."

"Mum, it'll be more than 'fun'. This is serious. It's a band. It's what I want to do. They're really good."

"That's lovely, darling. Listen, I've got to rush. You know what Julia's like."

The phone rings in the hall. Sylvia stares at the glass in her hand and pops a lump of cheese into her mouth. "Get that, will you, Jess? I'm going to run a bath."

Jess goes out to the hall and picks up the phone. It's one of those companies pretending not to sell things. The person asks how she is. Jess deals with it by saying, "Very well, thank you. Bye," and putting the phone down. She is about to go back into the kitchen but she stops when she sees her mum swig from the wine bottle. Two long, slow glugs. Jess feels sick. She has been trying to ignore this, pretend it isn't happening, that it's her imagination. Is her mum just drinking a bit too much or is she an alcoholic? Jess doesn't know when one becomes the other. She's never seen her really drunk. Or maybe once, about a year ago, but that seemed a one-off after a night out with Julia. But sometimes she stumbles or slurs a bit in the evenings and says, "Gosh, I'm tired tonight." There's been no sign of her drinking early in the day and that's supposed to be important, isn't it? Unless she's hiding it. But she certainly drinks every night. Quite a lot. Is it normal to drink from a bottle? When you're a middle-aged woman, not some kid trying to get wasted on supermarket vodka?

Jess doesn't want to have to deal with this. She shouldn't have to.

She doesn't go back into the kitchen. "I'll see you later – I'm going to have a shower, OK?" And she goes upstairs to her room and puts some loud music on. Heavy rock, which is not what she usually sings. It's music with power. The thunk of the bassline is thick like treacle, the voice a rich coffee, smooth and strong with a rough edge. It wraps its arms around her.

And she tries to forget what she has just seen.

CHAPTER 5
SCHRÖDINGER'S CAT

LATER, and after grabbing a very quick pasta meal while her mother's in the bath, Jess goes on the Internet before she leaves for Jack's house. There is something she wants to do. It is something she's wondered about before, but it's never seemed interesting enough to explore. Until now.

It's that name, Schrödinger's Cats. A weird name for a band. A weird name for anything. Who was Schrödinger? She doesn't want to seem ignorant in front of Jack, does she?

So, the Internet.

It almost makes her late leaving the house. Kind of fascinating, it is, but seriously strange. And to say that she doesn't understand is an understatement. What sort of mind can make sense of this? She hopes Jack's doesn't.

Apparently, there was a scientist, Schrödinger, who used to write letters to Einstein. They talked about a "thought experiment". Schrödinger imagined a cat inside a box with a flask of deadly poison. The poison would be released (killing the cat) if a radioactive particle decayed. And the particle might decay or it might not. Apparently, if you left the cat in the box for one hour, there'd be an equal chance it would be dead or alive when you opened the box to have a look. Just as in theory there's an equal chance of a coin landing heads up as tails up, was how they explained it.

Spike walks into the room at this point and curls himself around her ankles, purring.

Jess hopes Schrödinger never actually tried this on a cat.

So, obviously, the cat is either dead or alive. But Schrödinger said that, according to quantum theory, the cat is neither alive nor dead (or both dead *and* alive) until you open the box to look at it.

Which is freaky and makes no sense in the real world.

There were a whole load of scientists who had explanations for this, none of which made sense either (even to Einstein, which is a comfort to Jess). Even Schrödinger sounded confused, though he seemed to like being confused because it seemed to prove something exciting.

Apparently, the point was that this quantum theory thing was about particles so unimaginably tiny that even by looking at them you could change them.

To think that people get paid to worry about this

stuff. Seriously weird and pointless. *Though kind of mysterious,* she thinks.

Cool name for a band too.

Jess looks at her watch, leaps to her feet and checks her face in the mirror. Turns this way and that – darkness of eyes, check; fullness of hair, check; lips need gloss – done. Switches off the computer, grabs her bag. Gives Spike a stroke.

Ready.

CHAPTER 6
IN JACK'S HOUSE

JESS is walking to meet Jack. It's a simple journey and not much can go wrong. Of course, Jess and Jack will never know the things that might have gone wrong if they'd left slightly earlier or slightly later or taken a different route. Supposing, for example, one of them had been delayed by a phone call, or forgotten to close a window and had to rush back, or been asked to do a chore by a parent, or not been able to find a shoe. If they had been a minute later, or earlier, perhaps one of them would have been knocked down by a speeding car, or hit by a slate falling from a roof, or could have tripped on a loose paving stone, been mugged or struck by lightning. They might have breathed in the virus from a passing tuberculosis victim. Then how differently would things have turned out?

None of those possibilities occurs. They meet safely at the arranged time and place, walking towards each other with faces shy but bright. Jack wants to touch Jess, so he does, because he is not embarrassed about things like that. Jess loves the way he touches her, just on her arm, as he guides her across the road, safely through the traffic and in the direction of his road. It envelopes her softly, this new feeling.

A salty breeze drifts over them as they walk – Jack's house is closer to the sea than hers. It is a smell Jess has loved since she and her mum moved here a couple of years before.

Jack does not stop talking. In the ten minutes it takes them to get to his home, Jess learns that he is about to finish at the sixth-form college, doing music, English and philosophy; has a couple of university offers; is taking a year out first; but doesn't really care about anything apart from his band. He has one more exam to do but he's not worried about it. Will walk it, Jess gets the impression. Certainly, if he writes as much as he talks, the examiner will have plenty to mark.

He asks her questions too. In fact, he is exhausting in his questioning. Every answer she gives seems to fascinate him. He nods and smiles and agrees and uses words like "exactly" and "excellent". If you wrote his words down, the page would be littered with exclamation marks and capital letters. He does not walk in a straight line but spins round to look at her sometimes, or moves to kick a stone along the road. Energy sparks from him like static. He is mercurial, fluid. Quicksilver. She is aware that she likes him. A lot.

Although he is dangerous to know, she is right to like him. He is pulled firmly towards the earth's centre. Though he moves quickly, he has equilibrium. It is not a word Jess herself would use but it fits. There is a point of balance inside him. He could be pushed a long way and he would surely spring back upright. It is as though the double shot of bad luck years ago drew out of him all the loose particles that can float here or there and all that is left is solid and confident and fits together tightly. A magnet has passed over his body and sucked out all the negativity.

It will not be his fault if bad luck is round the corner again for Jack. Or maybe it will not be bad luck but something more clearly caused by his actions. Perhaps there is one moment where we can say, "No, please, Jack. Not *that*." Something obvious, like an actor in a horror film going downstairs in the middle of the night, in a storm, on Hallowe'en, *and not putting the lights on*.

"Anyway, here we are."

Jack's house is seriously big. *OK, so we're talking major money here*, thinks Jess. On the gravel driveway, a car sits, black and lean and low and panther-like. The gravel crunches softly and is unusually easy to walk on. It welcomes the foot instead of repelling it with jaggy edges. Sea moss and pinks tumble from stone urns. Through the window to the porch, a surfboard leans. *So, is he a surfer, then?*

Jack is turning his key in the front door and opening it. He calls to his dad but there is no answer. The hall is bright, halogen and chrome coming from the huge kitchen that she can see to the right. Jess takes everything in, with difficulty. She feels like an intruder. Maybe she should be quiet in this house, so smooth and elegant, so clean and shiny and with an enormous bowl of pink and white roses on a table, which she thinks is mahogany. Jack throws his key on another table and goes back to the door to pull her in. He guesses what she is thinking.

"Yes, I know" – he says, with that smile – "it's a beautiful house. Yes, I know – I'm very lucky. Et cetera, et cetera. Now, do you want a drink?"

"Um, yeah." Her lips have stopped moving properly.

"What?"

"What do you have?" *Like, is this a tea/coffee situation or some other drink altogether?*

"We have everything."

Yes, you probably do, thinks Jess. "What are you having?" she asks.

"Lime and sparkling water."

"I'll have that too."

"Want something in it?"

"No, thanks." Actually, she kind of does but she is confused. This whole place. This situation. Her senses are overstretched. She'd probably need a drink before she could have a drink in a place like this.

"Not while we're working?" he says. She gives him a look.

He begins to lead her upstairs.

A man comes out of a room downstairs and they both turn round at his voice. "Jack? Sorry, I was on the phone when I heard you come in."

"Hi, Dad. This is Jess. I told you I'd find a singer. Well, here she is. Jess, my dad. Dad, Jess."

Jack's dad comes up the stairs and shakes her hand. It's a firm handshake. A nice smile, the blue eyes friendly, the skin tanned. She smiles back as best she can and says hello. She knows he's searching her face to see what he finds there, whether he approves. Her mother does it to any boys she's ever been seen with. "Pleased to meet you, Jess," he says and he looks pleased too. "Hope you can help Jack out – he's talked about nothing but band problems – and if you can stop him talking about it you're welcome to him. Oh, and I'm Sam, by the way."

And he walks back down the wide staircase and disappears into the kitchen. Jess follows Jack up some more stairs, narrower this time. At the top, there's a small landing and two doors. He opens one and leads her in. She is overwhelmed by impressions. It's a huge loft space with beams. Lots of sloping ceilings. Dark, but in a warm way, with deep-blue walls, until he turns on one switch and different lights come on, and alcoves come to life. He has a double bed, which she doesn't want to look at. A lot of books. A seriously professional keyboard and a guitar, amps, other stuff with leads all over the place. The room is cluttered but organized. It's not tidy but there are no horrible things like dirty underwear or brown apple cores. Mind you, he's had time to tidy it. This could all be an act. He could in fact be a slob who has been well enough brought up to know that if you want to impress a girl you get rid of dirty underwear and apple cores before you invite her to your room.

She feels suddenly nervous. Soon she will have to sing for him. He puts the drinks on a table.

"Have a seat," he says. "Catch." He throws a cardboard folder towards her and she catches it. There are pieces of hand-written sheet music inside. She takes one out. He's extricating a guitar from a tangle of wires. Looks like a decent piece of kit. And he's plugging his keyboard into the amp. He clearly knows what he's doing.

"What does your dad do?" She's playing for time.

"He runs his own business, at home. It's…"

But Jess is not listening. It's the music she's reading. It has caught her. She touches the notes on the page and something flows through her fingers. She finds herself humming it, not caring any more that he may be listening. She hardly knows what she's doing, just immerses herself in the colours. For it does have colours, each blending into another, but she does not quite *see* the different tones, more *feels* them. They are deep within, where she cannot see, like tastes, melting together. They are, perhaps, nothing more than emotions, but they feel like much more. She loves it when music does this. She craves the weird letting go of it.

As the tune becomes familiar, she can add some of

the words, and her voice becomes round and whole and warm and butter rich.

She is aware of music coming from the keyboard, joining her. There is a bassline now, adding depth to the colours, which slowly sink to the pit of her stomach and into her legs, weakening them. She wants to cry but she will not. She allows every part of her body to flow into the music and the hairs on the back of her neck stand up. Cold, suddenly, she feels.

The song comes to an end. A bee is buzzing in the window. There is traffic in the distance. And the sound of surf breaking. Her mouth is dry. She takes a mouthful of her drink. Lets a long breath out.

He is watching her. Not moving. His hands are frozen above the keyboard and she thinks he has not played the last few notes, or even lines.

"How do you do that?" he asks.

"I love the song. Did you write it?"

"Yes, but I've never heard it like that. You are … brilliant."

His words clutch at her insides. "I love the song. Honestly."

He runs his finger through his hair, shakes his head, removing the spell. "Well, that's lucky, because you could get seriously bored with it in the next two weeks. And you've got another twelve or something to learn."

Forty minutes or more later and they take a break. Jess stays in his room while Jack goes downstairs to get something for them to eat and drink. At first, she starts to work on some lines of a song, but she soon stops. She begins to grin. She lies back on the bed and spreads her arms beside her, sinking into the duvet. She could lie here for ever, but she had better not. It wouldn't do for Jack to get the wrong idea.

She wants to know more about Jack. Everything, if possible. Preferably not if it's something she doesn't like, but she will take that risk. Perhaps she has no choice, though it does feel like a choice. She gets up and wanders around the room, looking at the books on his shelves, pictures on his walls, photos in frames. There's a photo that's probably his mother. One of his dad with a woman, not the same woman. Pictures of the band. She looks closely at those to see what the other members are like, but she can't judge anything from them.

There are all the usual revision tools – books, folders, scribbled notes and lists and things that have been highlighted. There's a list of things he's meant to revise – nearly everything's ticked off. Jack is clearly in control. His handwriting is small and neat, very round, but with unusually long tails that get tangled in the line below. She touches it. It tells her nothing, but she likes it.

One part of a wall is covered with newspaper cuttings. Dozens of them. They overlap, leaving no space between. At first, she cannot see the point, the subject. The headlines are things like "Lightning strikes twice for binman", "Not so lucky Jim", "Tragic toddler in donkey death", "Tortoise kills man", "Lotto bride's heart attack". *It all seems a bit ... gloomy,* thinks Jess. Does he get off on other people's tragedies? He doesn't seem like the morbid type.

He is coming up the stairs.

CHAPTER 7
JACK'S GAME

"YOU'VE found my collection," says Jack. He's carrying a tray with cheese, crackers, apple chopped up, a dip of some sort and some tortilla chips. A bottle of fizzy water. And two tall glasses with a good centimetre of clear liquid. Which she guesses is vodka.

"Yes, but what's it a collection *of*? I mean, what's the point?"

"Do you believe in chance?" he asks, putting the tray down.

"That's a weird question. Of course I do. I suppose."

"There's no such thing," he announces. "We call it chance when we can't see the causes. Like spinning a coin – it's not really chance. There's physical reasons the coin lands the way it does. Tiny things you can't see."

"So? You still can't make a coin land one way or the other."

"No."

"So, what's the point? We still might as well call it chance."

"Look at all these deaths. These people didn't know what was going to hit them. They had no control. Look – that man died when an eagle dropped a tortoise on his head; that happened to an ancient Greek guy called Aeschylus too. But he could have been somewhere else at that moment, just a little way away, and he'd have been fine. Something made him and those other people be there at those exact moments. We call it chance, but it wasn't really. They were there because of other things. Physics."

"They were certainly unlucky."

"Exactly, unlucky! Brilliant! You've got it already!" Jess feels faintly proud but doesn't know why. He continues, bright-eyed, obviously off on one of his pet subjects: "But luck just depends on your viewpoint. See this?" Jack reaches past her and picks up a wallet and removes a pound coin from it. He spins it between finger and thumb. It seems to have its own energy. His body is still. Then he slithers it through his fingers and she watches it move fluidly like a minnow in shallows. After a few seconds – showing off, Jess knows – he flicks it into the air again, catches it and brings it down flat on the back of his other hand, closing his palm around it. "Heads or tails?"

"Tails."

He opens his hand wide and reveals the coin. Head facing up.

"Bad luck!"

"Your point?" She is annoyed. She is being patronized, played with.

"No point. The coin landed as it did because of unseen but *physical* causes. Luck doesn't come into it. Luck is just how we see it. To the coin, it makes no difference whether it's heads or tails. To you it does. The coin just follows the laws of nature. We call it luck, good or bad."

"You know what I think?"

"What?"

"That you're pretty pretentious. And I guess if you're into all this it explains why your band is called Schrödinger's Cats?" She's going to show him she's not ignorant.

Jack stares at her. "You understand about that?"

"Do you? I mean, it seems pointless to me."

"I don't think anyone's supposed to understand it – I just thought it was a cool name for a band. We were talking about it in philosophy one day – about parallel worlds and different types of truth, but no one actually understood it. Our teacher said you can't understand it unless you're mad."

Jess is relieved.

Then he grins. "Anyway, about being pretentious, can I carry on? Please? It's interesting."

"Go on then. But I'm this close to being seriously bored by all this physics or philosophy or whatever." She holds her finger and thumb up, perhaps a millimetre apart. Though she's smiling.

"Here's an example. This. Me hearing you sing. I didn't know you existed but I *needed* you to. And I walked past that door at the right time. Past a soundproofed room. Where the door wasn't properly shut. Invisible things came together to make it happen. Natural, physical things. Not chance, but definitely luck for me." He's not looking cheesy when he says it.

Something stirs inside her. She's not sure what he means but she likes his eyes while he says it. He has one hand through his hair, holding it off his face. His fingers are long and flat and wiry. She'd like to touch them.

"The ancient Greeks used to sacrifice to the gods because they thought the gods would give them bad luck if they didn't. Sometimes I think you have to do something like that," he continues. "See, those people" – and he waves towards the wall with the newspaper cuttings – "they weren't doing risky things. Stuff like that could happen to anyone. But if they'd done something a tiny bit differently they'd be alive now. Instead of just falling into the day as though they didn't care. You have to care. You have to take control even when it appears that you have none."

"But how would they know what to do differently? If they didn't know what was going to hit them?"

"No, they wouldn't *know*. But supposing they'd of-fered themselves up, like a sacrifice. Supposing they'd tossed a coin that morning and asked it a question: Should I leave the house five minutes earlier today? Should I cross the road at the first lights or the second? Should I get a pizza at lunch or take a home-made sandwich? When I go to Northseas High, should I walk down *that* corridor or *that* one? Then everything might have been different. So they could have changed their lives, if they'd done a tiny thing differently. Like Buddy Holly's band member, Tommy Allsup. You know about that?"

"No, but I'm guessing you're going to tell me."

"Tommy Allsup was supposed to be in the plane that crashed and killed Buddy Holly, but somebody else wanted to go. Tommy agreed to toss a coin for the seat and he lost. The other guy died. If he hadn't agreed to toss the coin, Tommy would have died."

"Wow."

He passes her one of the glasses with the clear liquid in. "It's OK – I'll just have water," she says. She doesn't know why. It just seems to be what she wants to say, and yet she sort of doesn't. The words just come out of her mouth. Of course, she is the one who instructed her brain but she doesn't really know why or even when or whether.

"Sure? It's elderflower cordial."

"Oh, right! Yes, please, then."

"You thought it was vodka!"

"Well, yes, but…"

"So you don't drink then?"

"Yes, of course I do. But…" But what? Jess doesn't know. Is it an issue? It's like chocolate. She eats chocolate but she might easily have said no to chocolate. It doesn't mean she doesn't eat chocolate. Chocolate isn't an *issue*.

Jack gets up and goes to a cupboard. Removes an unopened bottle of vodka. "You sure? Just one?"

Now she's said no, she wants to stay saying no. Or she would feel manipulated. "No, thanks. It's OK."

Jack places it on the table. Picks up the coin, does that showing off spinny thing again, looks at the coin where it lands. With a blank expression, he picks up the bottle and puts it back in the cupboard. "Me neither." He sits back down next to her. "That bottle has been there since my eighteenth birthday. Someone gave it to me."

"So, you don't drink?"

"Actually, no, I don't, mostly. Except sometimes, a bit, when I want to. It's a control thing. Alcohol removes free will. Sorry, being pretentious again. I get like that." And Jack looks down at the floor and fiddles with a piece of thread from the edge of a rug and then looks up at Jess and she melts. There is something about him. There is a lot about him and half of it is strange but all of it is exciting.

She picks up the coin and tries to flick it into the air. It twists once and then drops like lead to the ground, where it performs a pathetic totter before rolling under a table.

He retrieves it. He takes her hand, and her heart tumbles as he manipulates the fingers into the right position. He balances the coin on the edge of her middle finger and places her thumb lightly beneath it. "Gently," he says. "Flick." She feels his breath on her face. She flicks, and the coin spins a couple of times. He catches it, spins it again and brings it down on the back of her hand, which he has taken in his left. He covers it with his right hand, looks at her and asks, "Heads or tails? Concentrate. Imagine the answer's important."

She tries to think. It's not easy when he's holding her hand, but she tries. In her mind heads and tails vie for position. She could say either. Which will she say? Heads? Tails? Heads? Tails? How can she decide? Her mouth has to say one or the other – it would be ridiculous not to be able to decide. But what will make her say heads? Or tails? Heads? Tails? Come on, just *say* one!

"Tails." It is tails. "Yes!" She is ridiculously pleased.

"Chance?" he asks.

"Luck," she replies.

"Exactly! So do you want to play the game for real? After all, bad luck could strike you on your way home. Or later. And maybe by making a sacrifice to luck now, you will avoid that."

"Well, I'd better do it, then, hadn't I? Wouldn't want a tortoise dropping on my head."

"Exactly. So, here's what we do. We ask a really important question and we have to promise to go with the answer. You have to put yourself in the hands of luck and then luck will look after you. Sometimes. So you see, if we get the answer we don't want, it's OK because it makes good luck more likely to follow. Probably. It's a kind of win–win situation."

He looks at her, sips his drink that is not vodka. "Ready?"

She nods.

"OK, here's the question." He pauses. The coin is rippling through his fingers again. His lips part and then he asks, "Will you kiss me?"

Heart flips. Looks down, as though shy. Well, she *feels* shy. She can't meet his eyes. Her skin holds its breath. The universe has two parts: there is the bubble of airlessnesss that holds her body, and there is the world outside it.

He is talking again. "That's the question. Are you prepared to go with the answer? It could be yes or no. Fifty–fifty chance. In theory. Heads is yes, by the way."

She takes a drink too. She wishes it *was* vodka. "Yes." Sweat is on her palms. There are footsteps downstairs, the sound of a toilet flushing, a door closing. She breathes, but only just.

He flicks the coin with his thumb, high into the air. They both watch it spin and fall into his hand, where he grabs it and slaps his palm onto the back of his other hand but does not reveal the coin. He has not seen it either. And now Jess knows how much she wants the coin to land the right way up.

It doesn't.

CHAPTER 8
IN THE MIDDLE OF THE NIGHT

JACK has walked Jess home. They do not kiss because the game has not allowed them to. But he catches her hand as she opens the gate and something snatches her throat.

"See you tomorrow," he says. It is dark but she can see his eyes in the streetlight. It should probably be moonlight but it isn't.

She says something ordinary. Maybe she says *Yes* or *See you* or *Thanks for walking me home* or something. It doesn't matter because it wouldn't make any difference to anything. They are now linked anyway and they both know it. Nothing needs to be said.

Of course, either of them *could* choose to say something that would stop this relationship dead. "Free will" should allow them to let any words out of their mouths. Like, *Sorry, I think we're making a mistake. I don't want to see you again.* Or *I am only interested in you for what you can bring to the band, by the way.* But it's not going to happen. Because although they technically could say that, the words that come from their mouths have to come from something that already exists inside them. Everything has a reason, purpose or cause. One thing leads to another and for now everything leads them to feel desire.

The coin landing the wrong way has only increased that. So, maybe it did make a difference.

Jack watches as she goes up the path and turns her key in the door. He sees her walk inside, turn the light on and wave to him. He waves back, stands a moment longer and then walks home. He reaches home safely. Although many things could happen, they usually don't. And for everything that happens, there are billions and billions more that don't.

On that short journey, he walks slowly, though he doesn't particularly mean to. Time has clunked into a new groove and there is more in the world to be sensed now. There are more star patterns than he thought and space is deeper and there is energy in every cell of him and the nearby chippy smells mouth-watering. Around him, the night is warm and close and treacly. He lifts his hand – the one that touched Jess's – to his face and then punches the air and all his excitement comes out in one word: "Yesss!"

Lucky Jack. He has a girl for his band. Not just any girl, not just the sort of girl you'd get if you measured the probability, or if chance was really random, or if dreams were in any way realistic, but *this* girl. A girl with wide brown eyes and caramel skin and a voice smooth and rich as chocolate.

Jess, meanwhile, walks into the kitchen and gets herself a drink of water, which she carries slowly up to bed. She feels alive. As though before she has merely been sleepwalking and now she is fully awake. In the bathroom mirror, before she removes her make-up, she stares and tries to see what Jack must see. She knows she must be the same as this morning, and yet it feels as though everything has changed, as if she's on the edge of something huge and invisible.

Soon, she is in her bed, childhood toys staring down from the top of a wardrobe. They are probably thick with dust because she has not touched them for a long time but she still knows they are there. One day they will no longer exist; it is not possible to imagine the moments when each will be thrown away, but for each toy that moment will happen.

Sleep is nowhere near. She gets out of bed again, sensing the carpet between her toes and her pyjama straps on her shoulders as she walks towards the window. The night is hot and thick and windless.

Something important has happened to her that ordinary day and she had not been expecting anything like it at all.

She thinks back to the luck that meant that Jack had heard her sing. And when she tries to take in the factors that had to be right for it to happen, when she tries to contemplate how easily it might not have, her mind is boggled and overwhelmed. It is best not to think, to take it in one's stride and just let things happen. Jack thinks he can manipulate luck. But she is not so sure. She wants to believe, but he could be wrong.

She's quite happy to go along with it though. After all, it's just a game. Won't make any difference. It's even kind of interesting.

As she's lying in bed later, not really trying to sleep, just enjoying thinking about the evening and all the feelings of it, she hears her mum come back. There's a crash of something being dropped, the door shutting too noisily, her mum cursing as she knocks against something. It's the sound of a drunk person trying to be quiet. Just one person – it doesn't seem as though Julia has come back with her. Which is lucky, since then there'd be double the noise and a load of laughing and in the morning Jess would have to look at Julia's large middle-aged body spilling out of the skimpy clothes she'd been wearing the night before and would have to remind her that no, she can't smoke in the house because that's the house rule. Julia would roll her eyes and look scathingly at Jess and Sylvia would say something vaguely irritating to both of them. And the house would smell of stale cigarettes and dregs of wine and residual sweaty perfume.

Soon, the house is silent again. Her mum has gone to bed. Jess wonders if she ought to go and check that she's OK. No, her mum should look after herself.

A few minutes later, there's a hurried stumbling of feet across the landing, a groan and the sound of her mother vomiting in the toilet.

Jess turns on her side, pulls the duvet over her head, and eventually blocks her mother out.

CHAPTER 9
THE COLOUR OF LOSS

IT is the following day, a head-rushing hot Saturday. It will soon be evening, when darkness will bring something perilous to Jack or Jess. But for now it is day and the sky is clear. Some things will happen that are not dangerous at all. Although perhaps all those things, too, are part of the whole jumble and you just can't untangle it: small things having huge and unpredictable effects, like butterfly wings in New York causing hurricanes in Indonesia. Or whatever it is.

In the morning, Jess had fed Spike and was leaving the kitchen, toast in mouth, tea cooling in mug, when Sylvia groaned down the stairs, gripping the banister with one hand, one finger and thumb of the other pressing tightly into her forehead as though she could squeeze out the pain if she pressed hard enough.

"Gotta go, Mum. I'm going to Jack's house – band practice? You look rough."

"Thanks. What band?"

"Jack's band, Mum. I told you. Anyway, gotta go. Don't know when I'll be back. Sometime this afternoon. Then I'm out tonight."

Sylvia made a noise sufficient to suggest that she vaguely understood this and had no strength to disagree.

Soon afterwards, wth the curtains of her mum's bedroom still grimly closed, Jess leaves the house, refusing to think of her mother, though it's not easy. A brief anger flashes.

The moment when she arrives at Jack's house is not one she will forget. He has come to meet her at the end of the road and his wide smile as he says hello makes her heart turn over. He grabs her hand and leads her into the garage. Jack's garage is large and contains no sign of cars. To be fair, there are two garages, and the other one presumably has a car in it, but this one is seriously kitted out for a band practice.

The fractional silence, as the band turns to see this girl that Jack has found, is something loaded. One boy lets out a long, low whistle, then comes to greet her from behind his drums.

"Meet Tommy," says Jack.

A girl with a nest of streaky blonde hair and black-rimmed eyes smiles at Jess from behind a keyboard and says, "Hi, I'm Ella."

"That's Chris," says Jack, and Chris raises his hand, and then plays an impressive series of chords on his bass guitar.

Jack helps her get her mic at the right level and asks if she is OK. She nods, unable to speak. He picks up his guitar. He wears a thick, red sweat band round his forehead, holding his hair off his face. Jess takes in his prominent cheekbones, his angular boniness and firm chin.

They start with the songs Jess and Jack practised the night before. Jess quickly comes to love the sensation of the others around her, all working together without edge. She relaxes into the feeling of singing with a band, and it is as though she has done it before. It is better than being in her bedroom on her own, pretending, or in the school music department singing over a backing track. This is so real it is almost touchable.

She tunes into their wavelength easily. Nearly two hours pass; the songs become familiar. She adds her own flavour to them. Sometimes they argue a little about details. All of them are serious musicians; there is no weak link, no difficult ego.

"What about your song?" asks Ella, at one point.

"What?"

"Jack said when he first heard you, you were singing something and you said it was your own."

"The Colour of Loss". She is not ready. She does not have her guitar.

Rubbish, they say. She can use Jack's. He hands it over. Chris and Ella sit on the ground. Jack steps back into the shadows. She has no choice. She fiddles with the tuning pegs a little. It does not, in fact, need tuning but she is playing for time. Tries out a few chords, shifts into a comfortable position, foot on a stool, leaning over the guitar. Tucks a strand of long hair behind her ear. Closes her eyes and takes herself away and into the song.

At one point, she forgets the words, hesitates, stumbles, but no one moves. The song continues. Although she wrote the lyrics, "loss" is not something she often thinks about. The only things she believes she has lost are her father and a hamster that died when she was five years old, but neither of these losses has seemed to hurt her deeply. Not in any damaging way. There are no scars that she can see. But everyone can imagine loss and grief, and her song taps into that. She is not thinking about the meaning while she sings, only the colour of it, the pearliest blue. *For grief can be beautiful*, she thinks. *It is not always dark.*

"I didn't mean to lose you,
I'd have done it on a different day,
If I had known
If I had known another way
I'd have breathed a longer breath
Walked a twisted path
Danced a slower beat
Laughed a softer laugh
If I had known
We had no other day.
And then again I'd say
I only need a sadder song
And you'd be gone.
For there is no other way."

The words on their own, written down, are nothing much. But when the music fills them and her voice gives them life they become stronger than all those things. When she finishes, there is silence. And then sounds of admiration. She smiles, blushes.

"You have to play that," says Tommy. "Doesn't she, Jack? At the next gig. On her own?" There is a murmur of agreement.

Jack is still in the shadows. He is bending down to pick something up. There is a long moment when he says nothing. Then, "Definitely. Let's take a break, shall we? Anyone want tea or anything?" And he leaves the garage with their requests.

Outside, Jack stops. He takes some deep breaths. Jess's song has corkscrewed its way inside of him. He had not properly heard the lyrics before, being struck only by her voice, and now the words have churned something deep in him but he cannot quite say what.

Jack goes into the house. He is on his way to the kitchen but in the hall he stops. Sunlight is shafting through a circular window halfway up the stairs and dust swirls in its beam. For a few measureless moments, he does not feel his body. He is outside, watching himself stand there alone. He sees everything as though he has never seen it before, although he has lived here for about ten years. It is shiny and beautiful and the house breathes a bright yellow air.

Suddenly, he smells the sea, the salty chill fishiness of

it. It waves through him, catching him unawares, and it leaves with a cold ripple across his skin.

A thought comes to Jack then: how would all this be different if his mother – either of them – had not died? And this is what he has lost, not his mothers, who are in some ways still there as part of him. What he has lost is everything that hasn't happened to him, everything that he is not, but might have been.

He feels so small now, a fractional part of something vast and unknowable. Because everyone, everyone in the world, has an equal loss. *Everyone* has a billion things that haven't happened. He is nothing special.

He shivers. Then walks into the kitchen to get what he came for. When he goes to open the fridge he discovers that his fingers are crossed. He looks at them.

Lucky Jack. How long will his luck hold?

CHAPTER 10
MEETING KELLY JONES

NOW it is evening and the forces of night are gathering. Of course, many bad things happen in daylight too and many nights pass peacefully. But not this time.

Jess has been home after the day spent practising. It had been perhaps half past seven when she'd got home and her mum had been nippy with her.

"I've already eaten. I couldn't wait any longer," Sylvia had said. And indeed the kitchen had shown signs of this, with a single plate and single knife and fork sitting there by the sink. Not the wine glass, for that was not finished with.

"I did text, Mum."

"Well, you know what I'm like with my phone."

"Yes, well, if you want me to text you it might be sensible *not* to be like that with your phone."

"Yes, well, if only everyone was as sensible as you, Jess, darling," her mother had said.

Ah, so there's still a headache going on, Jess had thought, but hadn't said it.

Anyway, she'd made something to eat for herself, had a shower, thrown clothes all over her room as she tried to find the right items. What are the right items for the first night of a new life? All the usual problems come into play when deciding how to dress for this ordinary unordinary night – mustn't try too hard, mustn't not try hard enough, mustn't wear something which will show sweat, must wear something that goes with favourite bag/ shoes/necklace, must show enough but not too much.

But let's not dwell on this, for none of it will make much difference to what happens. Jack and Jess will do what they do, say what they say, whether Jess wears the blue or the brown, the floaty or the tight, this or that. She looks great anyway.

At about ten o'clock, she is ready to go. She leaves her mother in front of the television. Sylvia has tried to engage Jess in conversation at the last minute, not because she really wants to know the answers to her questions but because she faces the rest of the night alone.

"So, tell me about this boy," she says, remarkably brightly for someone who only a few hours earlier would have described herself as definitely within spitting distance of death's door. She takes another large glug of wine and the glass twangs against her teeth.

"He's nice. You'd like him." Jess is trying to leave. "Say hello to Julia for me."

"What's his name again?"

"Jack. You know it's Jack. I must've told you four times."

"What does he look like?"

"Just nice, Mum. I expect you'll meet him soon. Look, I've really got to go."

"What time will you be back?"

"We agreed already – two o'clock, max."

"That's awfully late, Jess. I don't know."

"Mu–um – we've already been over this. Exams are finished, and there's no school tomorrow, and no one else will be going home any earlier. You don't want me to walk home alone, do you?"

Sylvia shrinks into herself and picks up the TV zapper. "Just be safe, darling, OK? You got your key?"

"Do I ever not have my key?"

"No. You're a good girl, Jess." *Oh God, not now, please. Not the weepy bit, please not now.*

"See you later, Mum. Love you."

And she does, love her. But she will have to leave her. Both now and later, properly. She knows this now more clearly than she ever did. Somehow, she will do it.

So, Jess is approaching the bar where she is meeting Jack and the others. She hopes he is outside waiting for her so that she doesn't have to hang around like a loser. He is. His body is very close to hers as they squeeze past people. She smells his scent.

Ella, Chris and Tommy are all there at a table in a booth and they greet her, making room for her. Everything is black and chrome and not at all comfortable. But Jack squeezes in after her and the fact of things not being comfortable ceases to matter. On the table, there's a pitcher of vodka mixed with something pinky orange and lots of ice and a few bits of leaf. Someone pours her a glass and she sips from it, but in her head she tells herself that she is going to be careful tonight.

Which is sensible, but sensible may not be enough.

She notices that Jack has a glass of the vodka+whatever drink, so the not-drinking-thing is more of a drinking-sometimes-thing. This is something of a relief, because he won't be judging her.

"Cheers!" they all say, clinking glasses together. "Here's to Schrödinger's Cats!" The conversation eases and flows. She finds out a bit about them. Tommy – who has a drummer's jangled hairstyle – is at the same college as Jack, and his dad is in the army and has just gone to Afghanistan. Ella works in a clothes shop and is saving for her own flat. Chris is looking for a job – he lives at home and is not getting on with his parents, who don't like him spending all his time with the band when he should be settling down. It's all normal stuff.

And then Jack swears under his breath. He turns his head away from the bar, as though trying to avoid looking at someone. He *is* trying to avoid looking at someone. Jess can't see who.

"Kelly," mutters Jack. "Don't look now."

"Kelly who?" asks Jess.

"Kelly Jones. You must know her. She goes to your school."

"Oh God, her. Yes, I know her. I can't stand her."

"Why did she have to come here? Isn't it a bit classy for her?" asks Ella.

"Everywhere's a bit classy for her," says Jack. There's a real edge to his voice.

"Not your best memory from Northseas High, then?" asks Jess.

Tommy looks at her and then realizes. "Oh, you weren't there when Jack was there, were you?"

"No."

"Ahhhh. So you don't know why Jack and Kelly don't *exactly* get on?" No one is smiling.

"No, but I don't think you should tell me now – she's coming over."

Jack looks at Jess with a plaintive *Get me out of here!* look, which is quite amusing. Jess is intrigued. She does not know that a moment is about to happen when it really will matter what she says.

"Jack Redman. The oh-so-wonderful Jack Redman. And his merry band." Kelly is now standing right beside them. Jack has not looked up.

"Ignore her," he says quietly.

Kelly is not alone. She is with Samantha and Charlie, as usual. She is looking as tartily gorgeous as always. People look at them, and don't they know it? Kelly herself is tall – well, they all are, but whatever each of the others is, Kelly is just a little bit more. Which is why she's the leader. Her long, straight, sweeping hair is the palest blonde to the roots. Her facial bone structure is cover-girl-perfect, lips large and soft, skin pale and undeniably interesting, cheekbones to die for and accentuated by the clever use of blusher. Bubble-gum-pink strappy top, stopping just on her navel, with flesh on show beneath it. And a tight little stomach with nothing bulging anywhere. She works hard at the being beautiful thing.

Her legs are long and bare. They are smooth, lean and flawless, beneath a very short white skirt. Heels push her centimetres higher. She's a walking cliché. Straight off the pages of a cheap magazine.

But it's when you see her face that you decide whether you do or don't like Kelly Jones. She could smile at you angelically, and often does at teachers, or she could turn you to ice with the arrogance of her sneer. To be honest, even when she's doing the angelic bit, "likeable" wouldn't really be the word, unless you were some rather short-sighted elderly relative taken in by her sugary voice. Or a boy who wasn't interested in "likeable" anyway. If beauty is within, even the most powerful torch would fail to find it in the furthest depths of Kelly Jones's soul.

Arrogant sneer is definitely what is on show right now, as she looks down at Jack. Samantha and Charlie stand a little behind. Charlie's skin is expensively tanned, with hennaed hair tumbling deliberately over her shoulders. Samantha is the paler version, razor-thin eyebrows arching over highly decorated eyes in an opal face, her hair streaked with gold and straight as paper.

All are slim, tall and very high-maintenance.

"Why, it's Charlie's Angels," says Ella.

"What do you want, Kelly?" asks Jack, not looking at her.

"I heard that there's some crap band playing at the leavers' prom," says Kelly, her voice drawly.

"Yeah," adds Charlie. "We heard that somebody's daddy persuaded Willow to let his little boy play."

"And how do you imagine he did that?" Kelly looks at each of her friends in turn.

"Maybe lots of money for the school library?" asks Samantha.

"Or something more, um, personal?" Kelly looks at Jack now. Kelly Jones has been watching too much television and she has the LA-bitch smile down to a fine art.

Jack's face shows his anger. He opens his mouth to say something. But Tommy speaks: "Ignore her, Jack. She's not worth it."

Then Kelly seems to see Jess for the first time. Something else crosses her face now as she looks from Jess to Jack, sees how closely they are sitting.

"Well, look who's here! Hanging out with losers as usual, I see."

Which is when Jess makes her mistake. "Drunk as usual, I see," she says. She does not quite know why she says it. It just slips out. It's one of those insults that can be equally useful in many situations. Kelly, in fact, does not look particularly drunk, but then the night is yet young and she may well be later.

But that is what Jess says and it is, by chance, the one thing she should not have said. Not if she wants to keep the forces of darkness chained up for the night. But then she does not know this.

There is an intake of breath and the noises of the bar swell around them. Over the smooth shoulders of the three girls, Jess is aware of other drinkers, laughing, shouting, doing the things that they do on an ordinary night out. And then her attention comes back to her own group.

Several things happen in exactly the same moment.

Kelly seems to grow another few centimetres, as she bristles like a cat about to fight.

"Uh-oh," says Chris, with a grimace.

"OK, bye, then, Kelly – see you around, eh?" says Ella, firmly.

Tommy sinks his head down and slowly bashes it against the table in mock despair.

Samantha and Charlie both narrow their eyes. Charlie puts her hand on Kelly's shoulder. Jess wonders what's going on. OK, it's quite annoying to be accused of being drunk, but there's more to this than that.

Then Jack seems to have had enough. "Look, Kelly, you asked for it. Off you go now."

"You bastard!" spits Kelly. "I said I'd get you back. And then I thought I'd forgive you, be big about it, you know? But if you've told your new girlfriend, then you can forget it. And it looks like she's not the only one you blabbed to. Can't keep your trousers on *or* your mouth shut, obviously."

Tommy pretends to have died. Ella covers her eyes. Chris looks at Jess and makes a face which says something like, *Now it's war and although it was technically your fault, you couldn't have known.*

Jack starts to get up, but Kelly and her cronies have gone. They march on their long, long legs over to the other side of the bar, where they join some boys who seem to know them and who buy them more drinks. Soon, they will leave, after a hurried and furious conversation, but Jess and Jack and the others will not notice. Or would not think anything of it if they did. Though they should. They should be very careful from now on. And they will need all the luck that Jack believes surrounds him.

"OK, so what was that about?" says Jess. Ella pours them all another drink from the pitcher.

The noise in the bar is rising and something's turning ugly over the other side of the room. Someone has spilt a drink and someone else thinks it was deliberate. One of the bar staff is calming the situation with some practised jokery. It's the sort of argument which could go either way, flare or fade.

It's not even worth thinking about, because Jess wants to hear the story of Jack and Kelly, which sounds somewhat more interesting.

CHAPTER 11
KELLY, JACK AND SERIOUS COMPLICATIONS

JACK twists his head to look at Jess and tell the story directly to her. "Something happened, couple of months ago. We'd all been out – Ella's birthday – and we ended up at a party in someone's house. Kelly was there. She was pretty pissed."

"For a change," says Ella.

"Hey, does anyone want anything else to drink? I know this story," says Tommy.

"Yeah, thanks – orange juice please," says Jack.

"Me too," says Jess.

"Anyway, without going into the sordid details," continues Jack once Tommy has squeezed past them, "Kelly started chatting me up and, as you can imagine, it was extremely blatant and yes, I know she's pretty and all that but frankly I'd rather be kissed by an eel. Anyway, I knocked her back. I don't think it had ever happened to her before."

"You should have seen her," says Ella. "Totally flipped."

Jess is thinking that Jack really *does* seem not to be under Kelly's spell. She likes this story more and more.

Jack continues: "I didn't think any more about her until I was cycling home after the party was over. I heard this noise in someone's garden. It was Kelly, lying on the ground, virtually unconscious, and throwing up. Charlie was with her and frankly she wasn't much better but she was at least conscious. I said we had to get help. Charlie tried to stop me but what could I do? I seriously thought Kelly could choke on her own vomit."

This is not a pleasant image.

"So I went back to where the party was and I had to get hold of the parents, who were next door keeping out of the way and not best pleased to have to be involved. And to cut a long story short, they called Kelly's parents and she ended up in hospital for the night. Then I think she was grounded for ages – oh, and she had to go and apologize to the people whose garden she'd thrown up all over. She'd puked on a gnome and the woman made her replace it. And *that* story made her a laughing stock too."

"And all Jack's fault, you see?" says Chris.

"And she's still pissed off about it now?" asks Jess.

"Ah, well, that's not quite all," says Ella.

"She accused me of trying to assault her, as in sexually."

"The cow."

"Stupid too – no one believed her. She's an idiot – I had witnesses who'd been with me all night and everyone knew how pissed she was."

"So, major humiliation for Kelly Jones." Jess can't help feeling quite satisfied.

"Exactly."

"I can see why she hates you."

"And I rather suspect that you are now included in her circle of hate. Anyway, can we please not think about her? She's not worth it."

Tommy has come back with the drinks. Jess takes her orange juice, but she also pours herself something from the pitcher that appears. Her mouth is feeling pleasantly tingly and her feet heavy, but she is perfectly well in control of everything she wants to be in control of. Jack leans towards her to say something but she cannot hear over the rising noise of voices. His mouth is close to her skin and she can feel his breath, see the lines on his lips. When he touches her hair to push it behind her ear, her heart tumbles. A cliché, but true, she discovers. Skin-tingling and all the rest.

This and other moments like it take them all through the next hour and it is time to move on, to go to the club, where music, more drinks and dancing are supposed to occupy the rest of the night.

Before they leave, Jess and Ella go to the toilets. It is very possible that Kelly might be there or might see them, but she isn't and therefore doesn't, and they have more or less forgotten about her. Which is pleasant but unwise.

"So, how much do you like Jack, then?" asks Ella. Jess grins as she says she likes him a lot. "It's obvious he likes you," says Ella. "I'm really pleased. He needs someone like you. He's great and everything but he can be intense and that thing with the coin... Well, he takes risks. You know? Sometimes it's as though he doesn't care what happens. It's like tempting fate, challenging it to come and get him."

"I know what you mean," says Jess. "He told me about the game thing. It seems kind of weird, but interesting. Kind of deep."

"Yeah, I suppose. You know about his mother, don't you?"

"I know his mother's dead but no details."

"Well, ask him. It's not a secret and he's quite open about it but he should tell you, not me. He told me once he'd had so much bad luck early on that he'd used it all up. He calls himself Lucky Jack, spins that coin as though he thinks he actually controls it. I don't know, but I just don't think it's right. So, look after him, will you? He can be a cocky bastard but we all love him."

Jess thinks about this briefly, as they walk back to the others. Jack is talking to Tommy and Chris, near the door, waiting for the girls. But all Jess can really think about is the feeling when he looks at her. If he has a hidden vulnerability then that is absolutely fine with her. Makes him all the more likeable, if that was possible. And it's not as though he's screwed up or needy, either of which would be a definite dampener. Jess has enough of that at home. She wants a survivor, someone who will run with her headlong into the future.

Ten minutes later they are queuing to get into the club. Kelly and her friends are nowhere to be seen, not that Jess and Jack are thinking about them much. Tommy is not with them – he's gone to meet some other friends. Jess is the only one who is not eighteen and she has the usual tension as she stares the bouncer in the eye and answers his questions about her ID. She knows it all off by heart now but you never know when they'll spring a weird question on you.

There are no signs that something is about to happen. No omens. No solitary magpies or one-legged black cats. No one walks under a ladder or breaks a mirror or spills salt. The idea might have come into Jack's mind to toss the coin to see whether they should even go into this club. And maybe the coin would have said they shouldn't. But the idea is far from his mind. Maybe this is the moment when an observer could have said, *Stop! Make a different choice now! Toss the coin, Jack, and hope it tells you to go somewhere else. Home, preferably.*

So, perhaps it is all Jack's fault. For forgetting to make his sacrifice to luck. And now the ancient gods are annoyed with him for that lapse. But Jack is in love – he is in no position to concentrate.

Perhaps if they hadn't been so wrapped up in each other they'd have seen Kelly peering round a corner, and watching them go in. They'd have seen her talking to someone. They might have seen her face, twisted by anger and vodka. But even if they had, it would have told them nothing and changed nothing.

We will watch Jess and Jack for a little longer and then we will reach a moment when either one thing or another will happen. It is not possible to predict which it will be, because many small and uncertain things will lead up to it. It will hinge on something so tiny and unnoticeable, so uncontrollable, that it might as well be decided by the toss of a coin. Some people would call it chance. Jack would call it luck.

So, here they are, in the club, the noise so ear-splitting that they must touch each other a lot, pull each other very close just to be heard. They are not complaining. Jess is feeling slightly dizzy and has had enough to drink but she's at that point where saying yes is easier than saying no and there isn't enough reason to say no.

"Drink?" Jack shouts in her ear.

"Whatever you're having," she yells back, and can hardly hear her own words.

Jack and Ella go to the bar, Chris goes to the toilet and Jess tries to claim some space for them all. She finds a pillar to lean against. For a while she stands there, her head buzzing. It is tiring having to shout and for a moment she wishes she and Jack could go somewhere else. And that she'd asked for something non-alcoholic. She looks around at the room, packed with people, a few dancing, but most standing, drinking, laughing and shouting.

Once they are all back together again, it's not long before Chris and Ella seem to see some people they know and disappear. Jack and Jess both guess that this is not entirely a coincidence. Jess catches his eye. He's smiling. She looks at the ground and her heart races. There's an urge in her, deep and hot, which she thinks she may not want to resist.

The forces of night are ready. They are watching Jess and Jack and waiting for the moment.

Jess and Jack talk – or shout – for the next twenty minutes or so. They are unaware of everything else, wrapped around as they are by the noise and heat. Everyone in the bar could have disappeared and been replaced by robots, or turned green; armed police could be wandering through the room; a man could be leading a tiger on a string. None of these things is happening, but Jess and Jack would not have known if they all were.

Then, without warning – because there almost never is a warning – the forces of night make their move.

This is the moment when events will go in one direction or another. There will be a tiny happening, unnoticed by all concerned, which, like the dirt on one side of a coin, or an uneven surface to land on, will make all the difference in the world to Jack and Jess and some of the people who love them.

Here, now, are the two alternatives. Only one will actually happen. We will look at them both and then play Jack's Game and let the coin decide. Will it be heads or will it be tails?

NOTE.

Only one of the next two chapters will happen. Then, a coin will spin and the story will follow whichever event the coin "decides".

CHAPTER 12
HEADS

OUTSIDE the club, a girl called Marianne is queuing with her friends. Marianne has a fake ID. It is her older sister's passport. She has used it before and it has usually worked. She looks enough like her sister and, in any case, passport photos usually look like a criminal version of someone vaguely like oneself when ill.

There are two bouncers on the door. Marianne smiles sweetly at one of them.

He almost smiles back. "ID. Please." Takes it from her. Flicks through it. Is about to ask her a question. He isn't sure he believes it's hers.

"Date of birth?"

Marianne knows that one. Dead obvious. She looks straight at him, and there's a confidence in her face that goes a very long way to convincing him. But not the whole way. He still doesn't one hundred per cent believe her. He's going to ask her what countries she's been to.

And when. So he flicks through the pages to find one with tourist stamps. There are a lot of stamps – this is a girl who has travelled. Or, if it's not hers, the owner of the passport has. He can probably catch her out. On the other hand, can he be bothered? He's turned away a load of people that night, done his job.

No, he will – he'll trap her. Might as well. He opens his mouth to ask her the first question. But at that very moment there is a noise over her shoulder and he looks up. It's a group of boys, rich kids, noisily pushing into the queue. They could be about to cause trouble. The other people in the queue are not happy. His colleague has just gone to the toilet, so he's on his own.

For a moment, he hesitates. It could go either way.

But you can't hesitate long in a job like this. You have to make snap decisions.

He decides.

He lets Marianne in and focuses on the boys.

Meanwhile, in the bar, Jack and Jess are standing up, showing each other photos on their phones. They are going to dance soon, but they need to finish their drinks first, which are on the table near them. Margaritas, salt on the rims. Jess is not planning to have anything more after this. She knows she has had enough. Her head is gently spinning.

Kelly Jones appears beside them. She is smiling. Pleasantly. Which is disconcerting.

"Hello, Kelly," says Jack. Jess watches her. Alcohol has slackened Kelly's mouth and various other muscles and as she leans towards Jack she almost falls on him.

"Steady there, Kelly," he says.

She continues smiling sweetly, her face centimetres from his. Traces her finger down the side of his face and to his collar. Jess watches. Kelly's smile is not in her eyes.

Marianne, at this precise moment, has met Ella and Chris on the other side of the bar and is chatting to them. This is much more important than it might seem. Jack and Jess are, of course, unaware. They have more apparently interesting things to concentrate on.

Someone knocks into Jack from behind and he twists round.

A boy grins, holds his hands up. "Sorry, mate!"

Jack shrugs.

At this moment, Kelly appears to lose interest in Jack's body and walks away. Or perhaps *reels away* is a better way to describe her erratic path. Jess and Jack look at each other and grin.

"Weird!" says Jess.

"Horrible," says Jack. "Finish your drink and then we can go and dance.

Jess stirs hers and knocks it back. Later she may half remember that it tasted somewhat bitter but it's hard to be sure, especially with the salt on the rim. And anyway, she has drunk it now. She follows Jack onto the small dance floor.

CHAPTER 13
TAILS

OR, alternatively, is this what happens?

Outside the club, a girl called Marianne is queuing with her friends. Marianne has a fake ID. It is her older sister's passport. She has used it before and it has usually worked. She looks enough like her sister and, in any case, passport photos usually look like a criminal version of someone vaguely like oneself when ill.

There are two bouncers on the door. Marianne smiles sweetly at one of them.

He almost smiles back. "ID. Please." Takes it from her. Flicks through it. Is about to ask her a question. He isn't sure he believes it's hers.

"Date of birth?"

Marianne knows that one. Dead obvious. She looks straight at him, and there's a confidence in her face that goes a very long way to convincing him. But not the whole way. He still doesn't one hundred per cent believe her. He's going to ask her what countries she's been to. And when. So he flicks through the pages to find one with tourist stamps. There are a lot of stamps – this is a girl who has travelled. Or, if it's not hers, the owner of the passport has. He can probably catch her out. On the other hand, can he be bothered? He's turned away a load of people that night, done his job.

No, he will – he'll trap her. Might as well. He opens his mouth to ask her the first question. But at that very moment there is a noise over her shoulder and he looks up. It's a group of boys, rich kids, noisily pushing into the queue. They could be about to cause trouble. The other people in the queue are not happy. His colleague has just gone to the toilet, so he's on his own.

For a moment, he hesitates. It could go either way.

But you can't hesitate long in a job like this. You have to make snap decisions.

He decides.

"Just wait," he tells Marianne. "You're going nowhere. Oi, you lot – get to the back of the queue or there's no way you're getting in!"

There's a certain amount of grumbling. One boy is held back by the others when it looks as though he might argue. The bouncer has the power and they know that.

So, he turns his attention back to Marianne and catches her out with some of his questions about countries that she hasn't been to. "Sorry, love, not your lucky night," he says, grinning. And she goes off with her friends to try somewhere else.

Marianne, therefore, does not get into the club. Which is much more important than it seems.

Meanwhile, in the bar, Jack and Jess are standing up, showing each other photos on their phones. They are going to dance soon, but they need to finish their drinks first, which are on the table near them. Margaritas, salt on the rims. Jess is not planning to have anything more after this. She knows she has had enough. Her head is gently spinning.

Kelly Jones appears beside them. She is smiling. Pleasantly. Which is disconcerting.

"Hello, Kelly," says Jack. Jess watches her. Alcohol has slackened Kelly's mouth and various other muscles and as she leans towards Jack she almost falls on him.

"Steady there, Kelly," he says.

She continues smiling sweetly, her face centimetres from his. Traces her finger down the side of his face and to his collar. Jess watches. Kelly's smile is not in her eyes.

Someone knocks into Jack from behind and he twists round.

A boy grins, holds his hands up. "Sorry, mate!"

Jack shrugs.

At this moment, Kelly appears to lose interest in Jack's body and walks away. Or perhaps *reels away* is a better way to describe her erratic path. Jess and Jack look at each other and grin.

"Weird!" says Jess.

"Horrible," says Jack. "Finish your drink and then we can go and dance."

Jess is about to do so, when her drink is suddenly knocked out of her hand. It is Chris, with Ella close behind.

"What the…!"

"I think your drink was spiked."

"You're joking! How do you know?"

"We saw Kelly talking to someone and then she came over to you and we thought she was going to cause trouble. Then this other guy was going towards you at the same time. And it just seemed all very kind of set up that the guy knocked into you while Kelly was talking to you. I couldn't see if she actually did anything because I couldn't see your drinks, but I wouldn't put it past her to have it planned."

"But that's… How would she get hold of whatever it was?"

"Kelly knows all the right people. You know her older brother did time for supplying? She would know how to get whatever she wanted. Could have been Ecstasy or any number of things. I don't even know the names of half the stuff people can get."

Jess feels cold. Though she finds it hard to believe that Kelly would do this. Chris and Ella *must* have imagined it.

"She can't get away with this," says Jack. "What did the guy look like? Is he still here?" Jack cannot keep still.

"He's probably left, if he's got any sense," said Ella.

"Come on – we've got to find him." Jack starts pulling Jess towards the exit.

"No, stop," says Ella. "I've got a better idea." And she certainly has, a devious and clever idea. Which she tells them. And they agree.

But she may not need to use her devious and clever idea, because we still don't know which of the two possibilities comes true. Does Marianne get into the club and distract Chris and Ella so that they don't see anything, or does Marianne *not* get into the club, leaving Chris and Ella free to keep an unintentional but useful watch over Jack and Jess?

We have to let the coin decide. It's time to play Jack's Game.

If the universe works by determinism, free will is impossible ???

"Nothing comes from nothing."

– Parmenides, approx 500 BC

Causal determinism
the idea that every event is directly caused by previous events and states and the laws of nature.

Schrödinger's cat
a thought experiment imagined by Erwin Schrödinger in 1935 involving a cat which is dead and alive at the same time, depending on a random event.

Weird!!!

"Life is like a game of cards. The hand that is dealt you is determinism; the way you play it is free will."
Jawaharlal Nehru
Indian politician
(1889–1964)

"I do not believe in a fate that falls on men however they act; but I do believe in a fate that falls on them unless they act."
G. K. Chesterton
(1874–1936)

VERSCHRÄNKUNG ("ENTANGLEMENT") – Schrödinger's word for what happens when we try to explain the ordinary world with quantum physics.

Luck describes the type of things that happen to you. Chance is an illusion: nothing happens by chance.

CHAPTER 14
HEADS OR TAILS?

THE coin lands heads up. For Marianne, the night is going swimmingly. Her fake ID has worked, by chance or whatever – she doesn't care now. Now, someone she likes from school has appeared in her line of vision. She finishes talking to Ella and Chris and moves on.

Swimmingly, in another sense, could be used to describe how Jess is about to feel. But for now she's walking onto the dance floor with Jack. It is perhaps not fair to describe in too much detail the sensations in their bodies. They are dancing together – how should we expect them to feel? It absorbs every cell of their bodies. It makes them hot, their blood surging, a melting feeling. Each move of fingers on body catches their breath, takes over their heartbeat, quickening everything except time, as the music pounds through them.

Jess is dizzy now, her head buzzing. She feels slightly sick. She knows she has drunk too much but it has come on her suddenly. Now, too late, she regrets that last drink. But she knows it's always too late by the time you regret that last drink.

And this particular drink – as we know, but Jess does not – is special.

The music slows and Jack takes Jess. He begins to wrap his arms around her and she vaguely feels his hands on her back. But she is not sure. She is slipping away, though her feet still seem to work. Voices, faces, head and arms swirl around her. The room goes dark and there is a salty taste on her tongue. There are animals in the room, wolves and dragons breathing liquid nitrogen, dancing. A unicorn stands in the corner, smooth and white, motionless, watching. Jess shakes her head but the unicorn is still there. A hunter prowls the room looking for her.

She is caught in a net. It is around her shoulders, her face. She tries to scream but only silence comes out and there is not enough breath in her lungs. The rope, thick and smelling of the sea, is over her mouth and she struggles, panic rising now. The wolves and dragons are watching her. Some of them are laughing. Freezing air washes her face and she gasps with a headache that grips her from nowhere. Colour has disappeared and everything is grey, darkening, now almost black.

Something crawls around her back, tightening. It is the rope, she thinks, at first. Until she hears its hiss, holds her breath, clamps her mouth shut. The snake weaves around her back. It is cold and oddly dry. It is on the bare flesh beneath her armpit, and on the back of her neck. Her skin creeps with it. She wants to scream and perhaps she does. Needs to run but can't. Jess tells herself she's having a nightmare, tries to shout herself awake, jerk reality back. In her head thoughts rush and tangle, coloured worms swirl through the black night and stab her behind the eyes. She doesn't know where the floor is, which way up she is. How to speak.

Her legs give way and her feet stop working. But she does not fall. She is being carried, dragged, by someone she cannot see. The hunter has found her. And now Jess knows nothing. She is not with us. She is nowhere. Her mind has gone to a place of such darkness and horror that we cannot follow, for our own good. It is best not even to imagine it. For Jess herself will forget.

Jack is half dragging Jess out of the club. How did she get so drunk so fast, he is wondering? Did she have more than he'd realized? Was the drink stronger than he'd thought? He has had more than normal himself, but he's fine, in control. He feels responsible – he's brought her to this club. One moment they'd been dancing and then suddenly she had stumbled in his arms and her eyes had gone glassy. She didn't seem to hear what he was saying. When people had started giving her weird looks, he'd decided to get her out of there, and here they are, outside. "Taking her home," he mouths to Chris and Ella as they leave. Ella looks concerned. He shakes his head, smiles. "It's OK," he says. He doesn't know if it is OK, but it will have to be. It must be.

Maybe she's tired, or hasn't eaten anything, or maybe she's on some kind of medication. Whatever, he wants to get her home, let her mum take over.

He walks Jess past the bouncer. She is limp, his arm around her waist holding her up, her feet barely touching the ground. Her head lolls forward, thick hair dishevelled. He feels the shape of her, the lightness of her body, but he will not think of that.

The bouncer rolls his eyes. "There goes another one. You need any help with her, mate?"

"No, thanks. She'll be fine."

"Yeah, well. Anyway, don't try anything on – remember, I've seen your face."

Jack stares back at him. Says nothing. Turns away. Something in him wants to speak out but it does not.

There is Kelly Jones, with Samantha and Charlie. Of course. They are laughing. Why are they there? At that moment? Where did they come from? And what is behind their laughter? These are questions Jack doesn't ask himself, not at this time, though he may later if he remembers to. He *should* ask these questions but he has other concerns.

Kelly weaves her drunken way towards him. "You know what, Jack?" He says nothing but she continues anyway. Her voice is full of spite and vodka. It is slurry and thick. "Your girlfriend should learn to sort her own life out before she accuses someone else of being a drunk." The others laugh again.

"She looks pretty sorted to me!" says Charlie.

"Have a good night, Jack!" calls Samantha.

Jess moans. Leans forward, retches. Jack moves her forcibly round the corner, away from Kelly and the others, away from the bouncer and from a police car sitting near by. She throws up in the gutter and moans again.

She is vaguely back with us now, and probably wishes she wasn't. She fumbles for a tissue from her bag and wipes her mouth.

"I'm taking you home, Jess."

"Don't feel well."

"I know. You've had too much to drink."

"Wolves. And dragons. I saw them." They're still there in the shadows, she sees. She shrinks towards Jack. He will look after her. Somewhere at the back of her mind she knows this was not how this evening was supposed to be, but she feels too ill, too strange, to care much about that. A small curl of shame hides in the pit of her stomach.

"Yeah, sure." He begins to walk her away, towards home. It may take them half an hour, but they won't get a taxi with Jess like this, and the night is warm enough. Sticky hot, thick air, ready to thunder.

"Were we at a fancy dress party?"

"No. We were at a club."

"What about the ucinorm?"

"The what?"

"Ucinorm. Like a horse. White horn."

"Unicorn."

"That's what I said. Amazing." She laughs. Then

shivers in the heat. Jack wishes he had something to put around her shoulders but he doesn't. He holds her more tightly, rubs her arm. "Come on, Jess, we need to get you home. Have you got any water with you?"

"In bag." She holds it open and he takes out the water bottle, unscrews it, offers it to her and she drinks.

"Don't feel well." And she doesn't. Thoughts and images are flying around her head like bats. Sometimes she wants to laugh and at other moments fear clutches at her.

"I know. You said. You'll feel better soon."

Jess wants to explain. She feels weird, more than drunk. She can't remember how she got out of the club. That is a time of nothingness. She has no sense as to whether it was a long time or not. And before, there is a horrible confusion, exactly like a nightmare. As though something had invaded her mind for a time. She can remember the wolves and dragons, the snake around her back, the unicorn which looked oddly like Kelly, but already she is beginning to know that none of that could be true. Though it still *feels* real.

"Jack."

"Yeah?"

She stops walking.

"Carry on walking, Jess – we need to get home." He keeps her moving.

"I'm not drunk."

"Trust me," Jack says. "You are. You'll feel better in the morning."

"It was different, Jack. Honesh." But she can hear her words blur at the edges, can feel her body unsteady, still feels sick. Which is exactly what she knows being drunk is. And her head feels thick and heavy, which again fits the symptoms. It doesn't take a fully trained doctor to say that Jess has had too much to drink.

But she is right. There is something else.

Kelly knows. Well, to be strictly accurate, she doesn't know what it is, or not by name. She'd just asked her contact to supply something, something − anything − that would have an interesting effect when combined with alcohol. And the contact came good and supplied exactly that. It was expensive. But worth it. It makes no difference to Kelly what the effect is. If sober, she would probably have said she wouldn't want serious harm to come to Jess − after all, the consequences for Kelly would be less than ideal if that happened. Police and all that. But Kelly is not sober, and couldn't give a toss what happens to Jess. She is thinking only of now, and she is feeling a considerable amount of pleasure at the thought of Jess throwing up for the rest of the night and perhaps hallucinating while Jack has his night out ruined.

And even if she had tried to look ahead, could she have seen what the consequences would be? She might have worried about Jess being seriously ill and ending up in hospital, or worse. She might have imagined Jess being caught by the police. She could have been a little concerned that Jess might be hit by a speeding car as she tried to cross the road in a spaced-out state.

No one, least of all Kelly Jones, whose brain is not of the highest quality, could have predicted the knock-on effects of what she did when she slipped a small white pill into Jess's drink. Or maybe it would all have turned out the same anyway. It's one of those many things that we cannot know.

CHAPTER 15
AN UNLUCKY MEETING

"REALLY," says Jess.

"Really what?" says Jack, humouring her. Her throwing up very close to his feet has not altered his feelings for her. It will take more than that, much more. Of course, he wishes he was dancing with her in the club right now, not walking her home so early, but he'd rather be walking her home than not with her at all.

"Really not drunk. Listen." She stops. She feels sick again. Takes out the water bottle and drinks several small sips. Feels better. Swills her mouth out and spits onto the ground. Fumbles more in her bag and finds some mints. The taste and coldness help. Now she can't remember what she was going to tell him. She swallows, breathes deeply. There's a wolf in the bushes and she fights to quell her fear. *There is not a wolf in the bushes*, she tells herself.

"There's a wolf in the bushes," she says.

"No, there isn't. There are no wolves in Britain."

"You don't know that." She knows there's no wolf in the bushes and that he is right. But it doesn't help. Fear invades her. "Jack, wanta go home."

"That's where we're going, Jess."

"Protect me from the wolves." She laughs. But she doesn't feel amused. It's just a laugh that appears. Bit like the wolf, not really there but very much there.

"I'll protect you from wolves. And dragons. And ucinorms."

"Unicorms."

He laughs. They walk on, in silence. Jack keeps a watchful eye; for what, he does not know. Not wolves, but anything else. There are a few people around, cars. No one takes any notice of them. He thinks about Jess and how much he likes her. Even like this.

Jess thinks about other things. She remembers something. "I was going to say..."

She stops walking, turns to him, pale in the strange half-moon, half streetlight, half not-quite-blackness. Three halves – he knows that's not right but *What the hell: we're not at school now.* He feels drops of water on his face. It is beginning to rain. Her hair hangs in seaweedy tendrils and she looks like something from a Greek myth.

"Keep walking, Jess. We're nearly home."

She keeps walking but talking too. "OK, I know I seem drunk. And yes, OK, I am. A bit."

"Quite a lot, actually," Jack says. Rain is coming on fast. He speeds them both up.

"Yes, but it's more than that. I felt really weird. Really. Really. Still do bit. Can't explain. But the wolves. And back there in the club – was horrible. There were animals and... Not what happens when you're drunk."

Large round globules of warm rainwater splash on their faces. "Jess, let's run – can you manage?" They run, him half dragging her, to the shelter of some trees. He pulls her to a halt, puts his arms round her and they stand like that, protected. A car passes and some young men shout from the windows at them, making crude gestures.

The smell of the rain is rich and organic. No other aroma is like it: in the whole world, only rain smells of rain. The sound of it rushes through the leaves. Jess tilts her head back and licks the water from around her mouth. Her hair is flat on her forehead. Jack takes a strand and lifts it off her face. With the tips of his fingers he wipes the rain and hair from her eyes. He almost cannot breathe with the beauty of her. He feels himself wanting her.

"So thirsty," she says. She takes the water from her bag again. "Really tired now. Legs like lead. Head. Need bed."

"We need to get you home, Jess. Come on – the rain isn't going to stop. Let's go." And they hurry on through the rain, Jack pulling Jess, and Jess just wishing she could lie down there and then.

He could have stayed with his arms around Jess in the shelter of the trees much longer but he doesn't. Could have kissed her, could have let himself go. But he doesn't. She is not well. He needs to get her home. And besides, what she said – about how she feels more than drunk. Is it possible? That someone has spiked her drink?

He knows, deep in his heart, that it is entirely possible. And if so, it does not take a genius to guess who is responsible. Or actually, is it so simple? Because he is partly responsible himself. He should have been more careful about Jess's drink.

There is a place of darkness in Jack's mind. It has always been there but he has become brilliant at keeping it shut away. By playing the game and following the rules of luck – he thinks – he has kept himself and those around him safe. The place of darkness is a memory, from a time soon after his second mother died, when people used to come to the house and help his dad. There were relatives and friends and most of them said the same things. Jack got used to hearing about time being "a great healer"; he got used to seeing covered casserole dishes and cakes brought to their house like sacrifices. He did not think at the time, of course, being so young, but since then he has wondered: did they bring those stews and traybakes as acts of pure kindness or to ward off bad luck themselves? There was a friend of his dad's at the time who did not call, did not help, and who did not try to come to the funeral because he was wrapped up in his own new romance. He remembers his dad being hurt about that. There is much else he has forgotten but he remembers this especially because the friend had been killed in a car crash on the day of the funeral. And his dad had said nothing about it. But years later Jack realized that if the man had come to the funeral he'd probably be alive now. *Wrong choice, mate. Serves you right.*

One woman he remembers, a casserole-bringer. Now he does not even know who it was, just that she had a flowery dress and a kind face and smelt of perfume, as he discovered later when she picked him up and hugged him. She was in the kitchen with his dad and they were talking quietly. Jack was coming down the stairs when he heard them and he stopped because he didn't want to meet another person. So he sat on the stairs and waited, picking at a curling corner of wallpaper. He couldn't hear their words properly but he heard bits – "playing football … so, stupid … I was always telling them" – and then one other word: "guilty".

Jack was not sure what this word meant. But the *playing football* and *stupid* bits were quite clear to his young mind. Something had choked him and he had run downstairs and into the kitchen and his dad had picked him up. His dad's face looked startled. The woman's expression crumpled and the next thing he knew he was sitting in front of the television and being given a chocolate biscuit, his dad and this woman talking brightly and loudly around him.

Jack discovered the meaning of "guilty" the next day at school. When he'd asked his teacher. "It's when you have done something bad," she'd said. Sometimes a bad person steals or hurts someone else, so we say they are guilty. And they have to have a punishment. They have to pay for being bad."

Jack did not know, and still doesn't, that his dad had used the word "guilty" about himself, not Jack. Because it was his dad who had put the long knife sticking up in the dishwasher. Perhaps Jack will never know this. But, to be honest, Jack has recovered. For a long time, he'd just felt bad without knowing why. And he'd grown up, become strong and dealt with life. Everyone said how brilliantly he was doing. Thirteen years had passed and that word "guilty" seemed like a nonsense.

It had turned into something else instead: *what if?* What if he hadn't kicked the ball? What if he had done anything differently, however small? Like not kicking the ball in the kitchen. Or kicking it differently. What if he had been watching Jess's drink? If he had tossed a coin, made a sacrifice that day...?

"It's this road, isn't it?" he asks.

Jess rouses herself. It is her road. She nods. She is exhausted, desperate to lie down. Her head feels like wet sand. "Number thirty-six," she says. And they arrive, hurrying up the garden path.

Lightning flashes. Followed shortly afterwards by thunder. Jess jumps. She fumbles in her bag for her key. Turns it in the lock. The door opens into a dark hall.

She finds the light switch. There is the noise of voices. Laughter. It's the television. Light creeps from under a door.

It is one in the morning, late for a parent to be watching television, thinks Jack. She must have waited up for Jess.

"I'd better go," he says. But he also feels he shouldn't. Or is that wishful thinking?

She turns. "Stay? Please. It's raining. And thunder." And sure enough, it is. "Come in and have some tea or something."

"You need to sleep. And get dry clothes on." They are inside now and the rain is falling fast outside. It has to be said that the thunder and lightning are only occasional and distant, but it is a storm nevertheless and Jack does not particularly fancy walking home in it.

Choices race through his mind. Reasons to stay and reasons to go. He is torn between them. He knows what he wants.

"How about we call a taxi and you have some tea first?"

He agrees and she starts to dial the number for a taxi, her fingers clumsy on the buttons. Why hasn't her mum come out of the room, wonders Jack? Hasn't she heard? The door remains closed, the television making a tinny sound within.

Phone call made, Jess points him towards the kitchen. "Just going to get something dry to wear." She goes upstairs. The bed looks tempting but she does not allow herself to sit. The mirror looks horrible. Her hair is matted around her face, her make-up blurred, her eyes wide and exhausted. She pulls off her wet clothes and tugs on jeans, T-shirt and jumper, brushes her hair, wipes her eyes. Gets a towel for Jack – she can think of no clothes that will fit him in this female house.

Back in the kitchen, she stumbles slightly with exhaustion. Jack puts a chair behind her and guides her into it. He has already put the kettle on, located the tea, two mugs, milk. Her head rests on one hand on the table, as though she does not have the strength to hold it up. She is still beautiful, he thinks. He dries his hair with the towel. So much for styling gel and carefully designed shapes.

"I do still feel weird, Jack. I was hallucinating. That doesn't happen with alcohol. It was horrible. Was I embarrassing?"

"You just suddenly seemed about to faint and you panicked. Freaked a bit. No, you weren't embarrassing." He is not entirely telling the truth. "Anyway, you should tell your mum you're back."

"She'll be asleep."

"But the TV's still on."

She stares at him. "She's still probably asleep."

"She must have been waiting up for you."

"Yeah, but if she's asleep she won't want to be woken."

He looks doubtful. "Maybe you should go in and turn the TV off?"

"I can't move," she says.

"Come on, silly. Course you can move."

"I want to go to bed."

"Well, you'll need to move, then, won't you? Come on, Jess — I need to know that everything's OK before I go. You need to be ready for bed and you need to tell your mum you're back."

"Let's take this tea upstairs. I'll get ready for bed and then you can go. Everything will be fine." The words are reasonable but she seems distracted. She stands up with her mug and sways a little.

"I'll carry the mugs." Jack takes hers from her and waits for her to go out of the kitchen. They cross the hall and she goes towards the stairs.

"Jess, your mum." He is standing by the sitting-room door.

"Honestly, I'll leave her. She likes the TV on." Jess is on the stairs now. She is struggling to offer reasons not to disturb her mum. She does not want to go in there. Really does not.

He hesitates, not sure whether to push her. It is not, after all, his house.

"Come on, Jack, I want to go to bed."

"Do you think you should turn the TV off?"

She stares at him, fumbling for words. Of course he is right. Of course, of course, of course, of course. She should go in and tell her mum she's back, tell her that she can go to bed now, that everything is all right, even introduce her to Jack. That would be normal.

But for all that she is exhausted, wiped clean by that

little white pill and more alcohol than is ideal, confused, brain-shattered, Jess knows. She knows what she will find if they open that door.

She could refuse. Jack will not argue with her any more. It is her house, her mother, not his responsibility. He will give up if she holds her ground for five seconds more. She does not know this, but it is true.

Or she could give in to his common sense. She could open that door as Jack says and find what she knows she will find. And what then? What will she unleash?

To open the door or not to open the door? That is the question. And she wavers. Yes, no, yes, no, heads, tails.

In one strange and wild moment, she thinks of suggesting that they toss a coin.

"Toss you for it?" she says, not smiling. She is playing for time.

"I'm holding two mugs of tea." He is playing for time too.

This is ridiculous. You do not toss a coin to decide whether you are going to go into a room at one-thirty in the morning just to turn a television off and say hello to someone. Part of his mind knows that.

"So I'll toss it, then," says Jess, and suddenly, strangely, it doesn't seem ridiculous at all any more. She comes down the two steps and takes a coin from the bowl by the phone, throws it in the air, making a complete hash of it.

"No," says Jack. "It has to be done properly. That

doesn't count. Anyway, you forgot to say whether heads or tails means you go in or not."

"OK, well, you know the rules. So you do it."

He puts the mugs down. Picks up the coin and cleans it on his trousers. Places it on his hand, with the thumb underneath it, looks at her. "Heads, you go in. Tails, you don't. And you have to go with the answer."

"Fine. Go on then." It feels strangely easy, this letting go of choice. Handing over a decision to fate or chance or luck or whatever. The coin will decide and it won't be her problem.

Heads it is. Jess opens the door and finds what she knows she will find. It is not her fault. The coin decided. It is better that way and she finds herself oddly happy about it. It is a relief.

CHAPTER 16
AN EARTHQUAKE CRACK IN THE ROAD

THE room is too hot – the fire is on. The TV is blaring. A black cat is curled up by the fire. And the woman who is presumably Jess's mother is asleep on the sofa, snoring. Her mouth is slack and open, her face flopping sideways with gravity.

That's what Jack sees. It's quite amusing, at least at first sight. What Jess sees is only fractionally different, though she understands more. And to her it is not at all amusing. Her mother is drunk, unconscious, and saliva is hanging from the corner of her mouth. She doesn't need to see the bottle of gin to know that her mother is drunk, not just sleeping.

Jess sees the bottle of gin just as Jack does. Or, to be more accurate, a gin bottle. For there's no gin in it. Of course, there may only have been a tiny amount in it to start with, but this was not the case. The bottle is on its side and this position lends an extra seediness, as though even the bottle cannot remain upright.

Now Jack understands. Why Jess's mother had not heard them come in and why Jess did not want to open the door. And it's not amusing at all. He feels as though he has stumbled on something he was never meant to see.

"Listen, Jess, do you want me to cancel the taxi? I don't want to leave you."

"What about your dad? Won't he be worried?" She is glad that he will stay, though what he can do, she does not know. She just feels that she would rather not spend the night with wolves, snakes and a drunkard mother.

"He's not expecting me back yet anyway. He'll be asleep but I'll text him to say I'm staying here. He'll be fine about it."

Jess nods, empty of energy. She is looking down at her mum. She wants to do nothing, to walk away from there. To pretend it didn't happen. To wipe clean the whole disastrous night and start over in the morning. She is so tired and she should not have to think about anything else but herself.

Jack looks around, trying to take control of the situation. "Turn the fire off. Maybe find a blanket or something?" They can pretend that this is just a sleeping beauty if they want. But they both know it isn't. Jess nods again and moves towards the fire. Jack phones the taxi company and Jess goes upstairs to fetch the quilt from her mum's bed. In her mum's room, clothes are strewn everywhere. Make-up is open. A lipstick-edged wine glass sits on the dressing-table and there is a kind of shameful nakedness about it.

Jess's lips tighten. Her head is pounding and snakes are not far away, still hissing in her memory. She knows the snakes and wolves and unicorns are not really there but they were, oh, they were. She saw them and that's all that matters. More than a nightmare, more real than that, a kind of madness in her. Her mother should be there to help her, not dribbling on the sofa. Jess is frightened by what happened in the club. What are mothers for if not to comfort with soft warm arms and mother-smell when scary things have happened?

She goes downstairs with the quilt. "Mum?" Jess shakes her mum's shoulder. Sylvia is lying on her side already, so Jess need not move her much. She mumbles and half opens her eyes. Says something that sounds vaguely like her daughter's name. Groans, dribbles a little.

And in that raw moment Jess hates her mother. For doing this. For not being there. It is a moment that passes quickly. It passes from hate and anger to sadness and anger. And fear. But although the moment passes, it is important, because it has changed something between them. There is a seesaw tipping-point.

It is a faultline between them now. An earthquake crack in the road. Not a chasm, though. It is small, crossable; they could, either of them, leap over it fairly easily. Or even touch each other from opposite sides. But it is there.

It may widen or it may repair, depending on many things. If Jess or Jack or Sylvia knew what the future held, they might try to make different choices. Or that is what they think.

CHAPTER 17
SLEEPING TOGETHER

A little later. Spike has been let out – ears back against the rain. The sitting room is silent, apart from Sylvia's snoring. A small lamp casts a soft glow, in case she wakes up and is confused. Confusion is highly likely in view of the state she's in. Though waking up is not.

Sylvia has, a few moments ago, been roused to brief consciousness – for Jess and Jack need to know that consciousness is possible. She has wiped her mouth, mumbled *Hello* and *Pleased to meet you*, fallen quickly back to sleep again. Jack has smiled at Jess, to show that he does not think less of her for having such a mother. Jess has smiled back, though she does not feel like smiling and it is a smile that is fragile.

This is not how the night was supposed to end: staring down at a dribbling mother. Jess is struck by the difference between herself and this so-called mother. She is glad her father left before all this happened. Though if he was here then perhaps her mother would not be like this. But how impossibly untangleable is the tangle of *what ifs*. Once the coin falls and life tumbles one way, infinite possible worlds become impossible. If you try to think of them too much it will turn you mad.

But when her father left, her mother did not go to pieces. She was angry, certainly, but didn't turn to the bottle. Unless she's been hiding it, Jess wonders, which perhaps would be easier with a young child than the near-adult that Jess now is. She doesn't seem to be hiding it now. Though perhaps it is actually *even* worse than it seems. Perhaps she takes empty bottles secretly out of the house and disposes of them. Jess has heard that alcoholics are devious like that. But deviousness has never been a Sylvia thing.

"You need to go to bed now," says Jack. "Come on."

And he follows Jess upstairs, after leaving the cold cups of tea on the kitchen table. Into her bedroom. She sits on the bed, shoulders slumped.

"Someone spiked my drink, didn't they?"

"It's hard to believe but I guess ... I suppose. We should get you checked out, maybe?" Jack is struck by this thought as he says it. Should they? But Jess is better, she's lucid, she just needs to sleep. Surely. And with Jess's mother in that state, they can't go now, can they? He stands for a moment, tired himself, struggling to think.

"No, Jack, no way. I have to go to bed. Please."

She's right. There's not really any argument. Whatever was in her drink, she is clearly recovering from it. It hasn't killed her. But he cannot think about that, cannot face that scary place.

"OK, go and finish in the bathroom. And have you got a big T-shirt or something I can use?"

She grunts, gets up, rummages in a drawer and finds something that will do. The smell of her invades him when he holds it.

A few minutes later, Jess is in bed, washed, make-up vaguely removed, or what was left of it. Jack comes back from the bathroom himself to find her with her eyes closed, lying on her side. The house watches quietly as he positions himself carefully beside her. He lies on top of the duvet, with the quilt wrapped around him.

"Goodnight, Jess," he says softly.

She smiles, though he cannot see this. "Thanks, Jack, for looking after me. And I'm sorry that … you know." Her voice is somewhat mumbled, her lips almost unable to work through tiredness and the after-effects of whatever it was.

"Could have been a lot worse," he says. And he knows it could. But just now, at this moment, in this place, Jack is only struggling to hold on to one idea: how lucky he is. Because if he does not focus on that one thing, he will be forced to face the other side of the same coin: that he was very nearly unlucky.

But being very nearly unlucky is the same as being

lucky. And lucky he is. Everything has turned out right. Jess has come to no harm. He is lying in bed with her.

It is best not to think of alternatives.

CHAPTER 18
AWAKENING

THE house creaks awake when the boiler switches itself on at dawn. Outside, the birds are singing after the rain and, as the air warms, the doors and windows and walls and roof click and squeak as though spirits were walking through them. As perhaps they are, though it is also the physics of particle expansion which cause the noises that all houses make.

Jack wakes first. His bladder is full and he needs to go to the bathroom. But he does not, not immediately. First because he is a stranger in this house and second because Sylvia may happen to walk across the landing at the same time and then where would he be? And third because he is lying very close to Jess, one of his arms across her shoulder, his lips in her hair, and Jess is asleep. This is a situation to be savoured.

A sound on the landing. Jack holds his breath. A door squeaking and footsteps doing what footsteps do.

A door – the bathroom probably – closing and soon the sound of a toilet flushing. Jack breathes again. *Good thing I didn't go out just then*, he thinks.

Wouldn't have made much difference, actually, Jack. Because Sylvia has just remembered that she has a daughter. She thinks, fuzzily and painfully, that this is an important fact for at least two reasons: because the daughter could get her a cup of tea and feed Spike, and because the daughter had been out late the night before and Sylvia probably should have checked that she'd got back OK. Sylvia knows that other mothers might do this. But Jess is more likely to check on Sylvia than the other way round. As indeed happened, though of course Sylvia does not know this.

So, Sylvia crosses the landing towards Jess's room. For a moment she hesitates. Not because she thinks of any reason not to open the door but because a wave of headachy nausea has just washed through her, not helped by having just seen herself in the bathroom mirror. She takes a deep breath to quell it, squeezes her eyes and passes one hand over her forehead.

Earth to Sylvia: don't buy cheap gin, she thinks. There's another, more sensible, part of her brain that says, *For Christ's sake, just don't do that again, you stupid woman. You're an embarrassment and you're turning ugly and wrecking your body, your liver, your brain and quite possibly your life, not to mention your relationship with your daughter. Everything, you bloody fool. Why would she love you looking like this? After all, he didn't. Just stop it. Stop it. Just never, ever, ever do it again, OK?* All of this is expressed in a silent internal groan.

It's in theory possible that she won't do it again. But it's unlikely. One thing does tend to lead to another and stuff happens all too predictably. Usually. It's the predictable things that should be so easy and yet are so difficult to control. The things that trip us up unpredictably can lurch us into a brighter future. Shock treatment. A defibrillator for life.

Mind you, a shock is what Sylvia is about to get.

She taps on the door and opens it. Someone gasps. It could be Sylvia, it could be Jack, it could be Jess. The moment freezes and Sylvia struggles to comprehend what she is seeing, while Jack struggles to comprehend what she might be thinking and Jess struggles to comprehend where she is.

Jack sees a dishevelled woman who looks little better than when she was sleeping off her gin. Jess sees this too, though she also sees that Jack is on her bed, and this causes her some confusion until she remembers why, and hopes she remembers all of it. Sylvia sees a tousle-haired boy apparently in bed with her only daughter. It will be several more moments before she sees that he is not *in* but *on* the bed and that he is fully dressed. Not that this says anything very important at all but she will do her best to hold on to the positive aspects of it.

Jack sits up. He wants to say, *It's not what you think*, but this would be a cliché. There is too much they all need to say.

Jess presses her hands into her eyes as though she could push her headache away. "Someone spiked my drink, Mum."

"Oh, *right*! So that's all right, then." Sylvia attempts to regain control. *Regain* is not the right word. Nor, really, is *control*.

"No, seriously."

"Yes, seriously," adds Jack. "I had to make sure she was OK, so I stayed."

"You say *spiked*? As in a drug?"

"We think."

"But, oh my God! Did you go to hospital? And what about the police? Did you do any of that? Are you OK, Jess, darling? How did it happen? God, I've always told you to be careful in bars. And I suppose you were drinking too? You should have woken me when you came in. Why didn't you?" During this she has been picking up things and putting them down again.

"Actually..."

"Look, I really need to go to the bathroom? Can I...?" And Jack gets out from under the quilt he's pulled over himself, at which moment Sylvia sees that he's still wearing his jeans, and very rumpled they are too. Considering that they are also damp and extremely uncomfortable, Jack reckons he's performed an act of supreme decency, keeping his jeans on in the circumstances. He disappears from the room and goes into the bathroom. He isn't entirely sure at this point what he has let himself in for but he has done nothing wrong, so he isn't worried. He just wants the bathroom.

"Mum!" hisses Jess. "You want to know why we didn't wake you? We couldn't! You were rat-arsed, if you must know. God, you could have died or burnt the house down or something. Not to mention that I was ashamed."

Sylvia is momentarily stunned but her alcoholic's deceit quickly kicks in. "I was waiting up for you, really. I can't help it if I fell asleep. And don't be stupid – of course I wasn't drunk, or *rat-arsed* as you so charmingly put it. I was just asleep. You should have woken me. I'm your mother – I should know if you are ill."

Sylvia is right about that at least.

"There was an empty bottle of gin, Mum. Lying on the floor?" Jess's hands are still over her eyes. The world looks marginally better this way.

"So? I'd hardly had anything. You're jumping to conclusions. And you're a fine one to talk."

"My drink was spiked! Don't you believe me?" And now Jess does look, because eye contact when you tell the truth is important.

There is a tiny hesitation before Sylvia looks away and says, "Of course, but, Jess, the idea terrifies me. You could have died! Do you know what it was?"

"Of course I don't. I just know that I suddenly felt really weird."

"Weird how?"

But suddenly Jess can't be bothered to say, *Wolves*

and snakes and unicorns. What is the point? It would just sound stupid.

Jack is at the door. "Hi, sorry, but could I borrow an iron?"

"An iron?" Sylvia and Jess say together.

"Yeah, it's just that my jeans never dried from the rain and my dad always…"

Sylvia takes Jack to the spare room, where the iron is. Ah, so they do have a spare room. Its emptiness glares accusingly at Jack, as though perhaps he should have slept here. But there are so many reasons why he didn't and none of them actually needs to be stated.

If Jack were to look closely at Sylvia he would see a blowsy hung-over woman of soft fragility, like some huge ungainly rose with the petals about to drop, but he does not look at her because he senses that it would be better not to, kinder to her and kinder to Jess. In some ways he wants to, because this is a mother, an imperfect mother, such as either of his might have become, but he does not, just sensing her dressing-gown and her lack of make-up, and guessing her headache and perhaps her shame.

She puts the ironing-board up for him. "I'm sorry," she says, "I can't remember your name. I think Jess told me. You're the boy with the band, I guess?"

"Yes. Jack. And I'm sorry you got a shock just now but we didn't want to wake you last night. You were fast asleep."

Sylvia looks away. "Long day. I didn't know when Jess would be back, so…"

Silence. She unwinds the iron. "You can manage?"

"Yeah. Thanks." *Was she going to stand there while he took his jeans off or was he to iron them on his legs?*

Sylvia duly disappears. Jack breathes deeply. Removes his jeans and begins to iron them. Steam rises with the faint metallic smell of wet pavements. Jess peers round the door a few moments later. She smiles and his guts shrink. He smiles back.

"Sorry," they both say together. They know exactly what they mean. Everything. And yet of course there is so much they are not sorry about, which also they do not need to say.

Half an hour later three people are in the kitchen pretending that many things have not happened and that this is a normal morning. Spike twines between their legs and each leg-owner in turn bends down to stroke him. A cat is a good thing to have around in moments of tension.

The humans have showered, washed their hair, dried it, mostly, though Jack's is still damp. Jess's hair is full and burnt-chocolate thick, Sylvia's is wound in a straw spiral, with stray bits. Sylvia is pretending not to have a headache. She darts from place to place in the kitchen, looking for things to make something that might amount to breakfast. She keeps offering coffee and tea and toast and cereal and juice and honey and yogurt to Jack, who is already eating toast that Jess has made. Jess's eyes are the only bit of her that betray the night. If you could look inside her head you would sense remnants of fear, the smell of wolves, the shiny spiral spike of a unicorn, the hiss of a hidden snake, but they do not show on her face.

Sylvia asks Jack questions, ordinary stuff: his dad, his mum – *Oh, poor you, how sad* – his band. And so life proceeds, shifting into its new groove.

Until the phone rings. Phones are often shocking things. They usually ring shrilly, and this one does. They ring equally shrilly whether the news is good, or bad, or boring or not.

Which of these things is the case depends on who you are and how much you care. Normally, Sylvia would look at Jess and Jess would go and answer the phone. But this time, because Jack is in the kitchen and his presence is making her nervous and silly, and because if Jess goes then Sylvia will be left with Jack and she hasn't thought of another question, Sylvia leaps to her feet and goes to answer it.

Jess, who is not interested in who is on the phone – though she should be – kicks the kitchen door shut and turns to Jack, rolling her eyes.

CHAPTER 19
ROCKING THE BOAT IN A STORM

"SHE'S OK, your mum," Jack says. He's not really sure if she is. In fact, in some ways she seems distinctly not OK. Just how OK is a dippy, chaotic single mother who passes out on a sofa with an empty bottle of gin? Is that mother behaviour? How would Jack know? But Jack cares more about Jess and is trying not to see problems.

And what he really means is, *I'm OK about your mum and I will either pretend not to notice or I will help you if you need help.* Because Jack is, as we know, charming and decent. If dangerous.

Dangerous? We've almost forgotten that. He seems so safe right now. The boy who brings the vulnerable girl home safely, does the right thing by any standards, cares. Irons his own jeans dry.

"You feeling OK now?" he asks.

"Yeah." And she is.

"You realize that if your drink was spiked we know who it was?"

"Yep." And they look at each other. Jack's eyes seem bluer to her today. His lips wider. Sunlight highlights the freckles on those cheekbones. He is very alive.

"So, what now?"

"We can't prove anything, so I don't see what we can do."

Jack scowls into his tea, swirling it round till it nearly spills. "She should be taught a lesson. You could have been really ill. Whatever she put in it could have reacted badly with alcohol and she doesn't know if you have any medical conditions. God, I don't like to think…"

"So let's don't, hey? The Kelly Gang are not worth it."

"You're very forgiving."

"Anyway, what about today? Band practice?" She's not really forgiving, just doesn't want to think about it.

"You bet. Band practice non-stop from now on." He looks at his watch. "When can you be ready?"

Jess gathers the dishes. "Five minutes. If you help with these." But her mother is back. And she is not looking happy. The words she uses when she comes into the kitchen and starts crashing around while making a cup of very strong coffee are not for repeating here. It would not be fair, for Sylvia is not herself and she has had an unpleasant shock. It is not normal for her ex-husband to phone the house.

"What's he done, Mum?" Jess doesn't need this right now, the inevitable over-reaction from her mum.

"He's only bloody coming, isn't he?"

"When?" Jess does not know what to feel. Mostly, she does not want to see him, not right now. There is enough going on in her life without the arrival of her father. Jess feels a stab of selfishness. Yet... She hasn't seen him for two years, when he'd taken her into London, no expense spared. It isn't that she is mercenary, but she doesn't hate him as her mother does. Just hates the situation and being in the middle of it and feeling obliged to please both of them. Being the glue that fails to hold them together.

And there's another thing. Months ago, when she'd been thinking about music college, her friends had said she should ask her dad about paying for it. So she'd mentioned it in an email. When Sylvia had heard, she'd been so unreasonable that Jess had ended up storming from the house and staying out later than she should have done. And then when she'd planned to talk to her mum again the next day, Sylvia had clearly been in no fit state. Jess had seen Sylvia snatching a quick gin. Was that wrong? She didn't know, just that it had felt kind of secret and dirty. And that was when Sylvia had started to show distinct signs of extra flakiness. And Jess had really started to think there was a problem with the alcohol levels.

Jess had to stop thinking about music college then. She couldn't ask her dad again, not if it was going to upset her mum so much. But she so wanted to. And much as she'd been trying to forget, the forgetting had only been surface level.

But now – what is so different about now? Maybe it's being in the band; maybe the bond with Jack is making it easier for her to stand up for what she wants, or making her more selfish – and why shouldn't she be selfish? Anyway, now she is losing patience with Sylvia and her flakiness.

"Couple of weeks." Sylvia spills the milk and curses. Jess grabs a cloth and deals with it. Though her lips tighten.

"Look, maybe I should go," says Jack. "Just come along when you can? Yeah?" Jess looks at him, shaking her head. The band is where she wants to be. Jack is where she wants to be. Her mum must look after herself. And her dad is not her problem.

"Mum, look, I have to go – we have to practise. For the prom?"

Sylvia looks at her, blue eyes childlike. "When's the prom?"

"Mum, you *know* when. Not next Saturday but the one after."

"But that's when he's coming! That weekend."

"Well, he can't! Sorry, Mum, but you'll just have to deal with it – that's my weekend and he doesn't get to turn up and spoil it."

"He's over on business, so I suppose that's the only time he can see you. Business, of course, not that he'd ever…"

"Well, tough. I have to go, Mum. See you later – don't know when." And Jess moves to leave the kitchen, leaving the rest of the dishes for Sylvia. This is not like her but Sylvia will have to deal with it. This is the least of the things that Sylvia will have to deal with. Surely she can manage some dishes?

"But, Jess," Sylvia wails. Jess looks at her. Sylvia is so quivery. She looks as though she needs a cigarette. Jess looks from Sylvia to Jack. And back.

Jack speaks. "How about you fix a time on the Friday or the Monday? Like, lunch or something?"

"Yes, Mum, why don't you tell him that? Lunch on Monday. I'll have finished school and I can go into town and meet him. He doesn't even need to come here."

"Why don't you tell him, Jess? Email him? You know how he makes me feel when I talk to him." Jess is about to tell her mother not to be so stupid but then she sees her hands shaking and a thought crosses her mind.

Jess turns to Jack. "I'll see you outside – OK?" She pleads with her eyes and he takes the hint.

"Lovely to meet you, Sylvia. See you soon. And thanks for the breakfast." Not that Sylvia has done anything. But she smiles vaguely and says something more or less appropriate back to him.

Jack disappears and Jess looks hard into her mother's eyes. "Listen, Mum, I need you to get a grip. Dad can come and take me to lunch and it's no big deal – you're just making it a big deal. And yes, I will email him and yes, I will tell him he can't come during the weekend and he can pick another time on Friday or Monday but you have to…" And then her courage fails her. How can she tell her mother to stop drinking? How can she hurt her like that? How can she step so far over the mother–daughter boundary? Besides, something is pulling in another direction – she wants only to be with Jack. She can't think about other stuff. Not now.

And so she simply says, "Don't let it screw you up, Mum. I love you but I have to go. Please just … just look after yourself. I'll be back this evening. I'll phone you to say when. But we can eat together, OK?" What Jess is really saying is, *Don't be drunk when I get back, Mum, because I will notice, you know? And I don't want to.*

It is entirely in Sylvia's control whether she does or does not get drunk. After all, can she not control whether her hand reaches for the gin bottle (supposing there is a new one in the cupboard, which there probably is, as alcoholics are good at planning ahead, if nothing else)? If Sylvia is in control of her arm muscles – as, of course, she is – she can do this. It's so simple.

But if it was that simple, life would be easy. Sylvia controls her arm muscles but she is not very good at controlling Sylvia. Maybe events control Sylvia and everyone's arm muscles. Maybe it will depend on who phones or what thoughts enter her head unbidden or any number of good or bad things. Perhaps if the sun shines today then Sylvia will feel happy and go outside and not think about gin. Perhaps she will paint and perhaps her painting will make her feel good. Or perhaps it won't.

All we can say truthfully is that she either will or won't drink today. It should be her choice. And it should be a simple one. So how come it isn't?

Anyway, Jess must go, for Jess has a life to lead and songs to sing and a love to live.

CHAPTER 20
CHANCE ADDICT

HEADY days follow. Jack spends sufficient hours revising for his last exam, but otherwise their days are spent singing, learning the words, growing into the new part, new life. Jess doesn't need to go to school at all now – practising for the prom, especially since music is what she wants as her career, is something the teachers are happy to allow her to do for these last two weeks.

For Jess it is easy, most of the time, to block out unwelcome thoughts. Her body and mind are invaded by a pleasure which easily outweighs fragile mothers and uncertain futures. Sometimes, when she is not with Jack, uncertainty forces its way back in and she briefly knows that there will be decisions to make. But she is happy to think of today, this week, next week, the holidays, and to let the far distance approach at its own speed. Her mind is filled with now, and there is enough of that to satisfy her. She will skydive and trust the parachute.

But Jack is dangerously tormented by a thought and a need. He feels too lucky just now: he has met Jess, fallen in love, found his perfect band member, and she doesn't even have a boyfriend. And now this other thing – that she came to no harm when her drink was spiked. He knows how easily it could have been different and how lucky they were.

Wrong. What Jack can't ever know is that, in fact, Jess was not *lucky* but *unlucky*. He doesn't know that she so nearly didn't drink the spiked vodka and that unluckily the doorman decided to let Marianne enter the bar, thereby distracting Chris and Ella, who would otherwise have stopped her. *Lucky* would have been if Marianne had been barred from entering.

Trouble is that Jack now feels a need to make a sacrifice to luck. Just in case. In case something bad is being stored up for him. Because he cannot ignore those stories that plaster his bedroom wall – about people who, if they'd done something slightly different, would have had a better day. Life instead of death. *If only.*

Dangerous words.

Which is why Jack is dangerous.

And on Friday night – with his last exam now finished – Jack gives in to his dangerous thought.

He needs to play Jack's Game. He needs to offer himself to whatever it is that decides. You can call it fate or chance or reason or mechanics but Jack must play the game. Because that is what has kept him safe from horror since his second mother died. He knows it works because it does, even though it doesn't make sense. It just makes a hell of a lot more sense than anything else – like why a small innocent boy loses his mother twice – so Jack will play.

He can, like Sylvia, control his arm – he can decide whether to spin a coin as well as Sylvia can decide whether to lift her hand towards her mouth. But, just as Sylvia cannot control Sylvia, so Jack cannot control Jack. Thing is: if we cannot control our own arms, if we don't make such simple decisions, then just who does?

So, at night, in the dark, after Jack's dad has gone to sleep and Jess is safely back in her own house having whatever conversation with her mother (sober or drunk, we don't know), Jack is going to play the game. He doesn't yet know what it will involve but whatever it is he will let it happen. However bad or uncomfortable or dangerous. He will give himself up to it. The only decision he has to make is to play – after that, nothing is his fault.

He has been lying awake in his bed, shadows around him, watching him. And now he gets up. The moon should be allowed to see what he is about to do, so he opens the curtains. Surely, if a moon can affect tides, then it can affect the minuscule currents and mechanics that make a coin fall one way or the other?

He takes his coin from the special section in his wallet where he keeps it safe, breathes on it and holds it to the moonlight, offering it. Closes his eyes and thinks for a moment and then says out loud, "Heads is left and tails is right." He looks at his watch. Half past midnight.

He will allow one hour. Anything could happen in one hour and there is enough risk in that to satisfy any god or spirit or whatever he is sacrificing himself to.

He puts on dark clothes, takes a torch from a drawer and checks the battery. His face looks hollow in the mirror. His breathing is shallow and he feels a little light-headed. There on the bed is the T-shirt he borrowed from Jess. He looks away from it. As though he doesn't want to feel watched by her now.

Quietly, Jack leaves the house, stepping carefully along the grass edges of the path so as not to scrunch the gravel. He slips out of the drive and goes to the corner of the main road.

The moon is not full but it is bright. Streetlights bathe the road, and recent rain shines in puddles. The sea smell is salty strong tonight. There is not enough darkness to be afraid and Jack is not. Though perhaps his heart beats a little fast. But he is smiling too, his body lithe and strong and ready. If he does not do this, then the next few days may turn out differently. Or what happens tonight may have no effect – he may go on his journey and return an hour later without anything happening that would seem to affect tomorrow. Jack will not even know one way or the other. For even if nothing dramatic happens tonight, he may wake later or earlier or in a different mood and therefore what happens tomorrow may be different from what would have happened. He may make different decisions without even knowing it. This he understands and trusts. He does not want any choice or responsibility, other than choosing to spin the coin.

At the corner, Jack stops. Left or right? The coin will tell him. He takes it from his pocket and breathes on it. (Even this could change its spin.) Strokes it, whispers inside his head, *I will do all you say.*

Balances it on his thumb, positions the tip of the thumb beneath his forefinger, readies his muscles to provide a certain amount of spin, not too much and not too little. Spins, loves watching it spiral, senses it seem to hang in the air before twisting down. He catches it, closes his fist around it and slaps it down on the back of his hand.

Heads. He walks to the left, striding out, breathing in the smoky night air, smelling cats' piss and rain. Spins the coin at the next corner, and the next, not even looking where he's going, just doing it. It's like playing music: you can think about the notes, plan your route through the tune, or you can lose yourself. Jack is losing himself. And how good it feels, letting go.

Jack moves from street to street. Most windows are dark and the curtains closed. Hardly anyone is about. On one corner, he passes a man and woman but they barely notice him. He looks purposeful, and if they saw him stop to spin the coin, they did not seem to think this strange. Or perhaps they think it is so strange that they wish to avoid him. At the back of his mind, he knows where he is, but he is not letting himself think about it too much. He is heading towards what his dad calls a "difficult" area. Some houses are boarded up. The patches of grass are scraggy and woven with shredded crisp packets, cigarette butts, cans, dog shit.

This street is entirely empty, silent, with only grey shapes of walls and bins and ripped posters and metal grilles on scruffy shops. A fox slinks across the road and he stops to watch it. Its eyes turn to him, yellow green in the streetlight. Why are foxes always smaller than you think they should be? More like cats than dogs.

It disappears behind a low wall and there is the clatter of something metal, like a bin lid tumbling. When Jack looks back to the street again, two men are walking towards him, on the same side of the road. They take up the whole width of the pavement. He will have to walk around them. Their hands are loose by their sides. One puts his hand in a pocket. Jack tenses, his heart thumping, blood rushing in his head. He veers very slightly towards the road so that they can see which way he is going. Part of him takes in the fact that he can see no one else. Another part wonders who would come if he screamed. Another stupid part wonders at exactly which point he should scream. It would be embarrassing to scream before anything has happened, but what if he leaves it too late?

He does not meet their eyes as they approach. He walks strongly, as if unafraid, but every muscle is ready to react. They continue occupying the whole pavement. It's obvious they are not about to give way. The one with the hand in his pocket now has his hand out of his pocket and it looks to Jack as though there is something in it.

This is why you came, Jack. It had to be dangerous; you had to take a risk. And you have to deal with what happens. That's the whole point.

"You lost, mate?"

"Nah, my dad's meeting me at the next street." It doesn't sound very likely, but it's the best he can do.

"Yeah, right!"

Jack cannot avoid looking at their faces. They are big men with big faces and big necks. One has a tattoo on his neck. They are smiling, but this may mean nothing. Jack doesn't have time to think. One of them lunges at him with both hands and Jack leaps back. His foot slips off the edge of the pavement and he feels himself falling into the road. Now everything is automatic. Jack's arms fling themselves out and every muscle in his back and sides clenches instantly to save him from falling. And sure enough, he does not fall, though he almost does. Gravity loses out and Jack just stays on his feet.

The men are laughing. He waits for them to lunge again, but they do not. Jack is standing there, hands in front of him, ready to fight, but nothing is happening.

"Don't trip now!" says one man.

"Or at least send us a postcard," says the other.

"Hey, Trevor, I think the boy thought you were going to attack him."

"Me? Doesn't he know they call me Pussy-cat?"

Thoughts flash like gunshot through Jack's mind – too fast to trace. But he feels, dares to feel, that perhaps they mean him no harm.

And then he realizes something – this thought hits him in the guts: the coin is not in his hand. He must have dropped it when he nearly fell. He looks down, quickly, aside, behind them, into the road.

"You lost something?" It's tattoo man. The tattoo is a woman with long snaky hair, twisting up his neck from under his white T-shirt.

"No," says Jack. But of course he has. It's obvious. And he can see it now. There it is, sitting in the dirt near by.

The men peer down at it.

"Pound, Trevor. See that? What could we do with a pound?"

"Not a lot, not in this day and age."

"Look," says Jack, "I need to go. Could I just have it back please?"

"Oh, is it yours? I didn't see you drop it. Did you, Trevor?"

"Nope. Finders keepers."

"Or we could give it to charity, or something, couldn't we?"

"It's my bus fare," says Jack.

"Thing is: you missed the last bus."

"Night bus."

"Not near here there isn't. Shame. But never mind, you're meeting your dad, so you don't need your bus fare, does he, Jase?"

"Daddy will come good," says the one called Jase, which is short for Jason, Jack assumes.

"Look, I really need to go. So, if you don't mind…" And Jack takes a step forward and stoops towards the coin.

Would it have made any difference if he had done the sensible thing? The sensible thing, of course, would be to forget the coin, which he doesn't really need, and just go. But this is Jack's coin and it means more to him than a pound. It was not the first coin he ever used, of course, but over many months it has come to have power. It is soft and loved and well worn and smooth and shiny and exactly right. If he plays the game with another coin, everything that will happen might be different. No two coins are the same. Equally unpredictable but not the same. Jack needs this coin, needs it with a gut-clutching feeling, a feeling that is without logic and is stronger than that. The same sort of feeling that makes us live our lives as though we have choice. Because we absolutely must. There is no choice about that.

Trevor's heavy boot moves fast, slaps down on the coin. Jason steps forward and pushes Jack backwards. Jack stumbles but rights himself. What rushes through his body is not fear or anger but something without name, something that invades at moments of extreme danger, something between panic and passion.

He stands up, as tall as he can. Holds out his hand. Asks for his coin back, in a calm voice. Even says *please*. Jack will do anything to get that coin back. He thinks.

Trevor now bends to retrieve the coin from under his boot. Picks it up in a huge stubby hand. Tiny it looks, glinting between those sausage fingers. He holds it out, slightly towards Jack. Jack reaches forward. Trevor snatches it higher.

"Look, just give it back!" says Jack, angry now, and not thinking properly. Forgetting that there are two of them. He is, perhaps, lulled into the belief that these men are only teasing, that they mean no harm and that this is harmless playground stuff. Stand up to bullies, everyone is told.

Trevor laughs. "Going to come and get it, then? How much do you really need it, posh boy? Sounds as though there's more where this came from, I'd say." And he holds it higher still. Jack will have to stretch tall. He does. But Trevor, laughing again, passes it to Jason.

Jason's eyes are nasty. There is no laughter in his voice as he says, "Yes, rich kid – come and get it. If you dare."

And that's when Jack sees what Jason has in his hand.

CHAPTER 21
METAL IN THE MOONLIGHT

A knife. Long. Slightly curved. Pointing towards Jack's stomach.

His breath freezes. He cannot take his eyes off the knife. It is half an arm's length from him. It is utterly still, watching him like a snake. He does not move, cannot move.

"So," says Jason, softly. "You don't want it now? It's here, if you really want it. But if you don't, we'll find a charity for it. Won't we, Trevor?"

"Like, maybe we could give it to Craig's fund."

"Good idea. You don't know our friend Craig, do you?" Jason's eyes are steady on Jack's face. Jack shakes his head. "He gets out of the slammer next week. Murder."

"Should never've been murder though – pure accident."

"Yeah, pure accident that Kenny made him angry."

"Exactly. How was Craig to know that Kenny was going to make him angry? Kenny should've known better."

"Let's hope this kid's not going to make you angry, Jase."

"Oh, he's not, Trevor. He's really not."

Jason is right. Jack has no intention of making them angry. The knife has turned his stomach to water. All he wants is to get away. The part of him that cares about the coin is silent now.

He backs away, slowly, very slowly, his hands steady in front of him, palms open, the instinctive sign of submission. The knife does not waver. Jack is now almost out of reach, and still the knife hasn't moved. Jack is ready to leap either way if necessary.

His mouth is dry, his tongue sticking to the top of his mouth. But he has to speak. "I'm sorry," he says. "Can I go?"

"You mean Craig can have the coin? You are donating it to his fund?"

Jack nods.

Trevor smiles. "That's very decent of you, old chap. Craig will be pleased. Won't he, Jase?"

"Thoroughly delighted. We'll have to tell him, won't we, Trevor? He might even want to come and thank the kid himself. Would you like that, kid?"

Jack says nothing.

"Answer!" snaps Jason, eyes narrowing.

"No, it's OK," says Jack.

The men laugh. "He doesn't want Craig to come and visit him! I wonder why," says Jason.

A police siren jars in the distance. The men don't flinch. Silence settles between them all for a few seconds. Can Jack go? He is about to ask when, without warning, Jason's hand lashes out and the knife slices the air in front of him. Jack gasps and flings himself backwards, landing heavily on the ground. Pain shoots up his back but he tries not to wince.

He looks up. He is not resigned to what will happen but his mind has stopped and there is nothing his body can do. Power is with the two men. Jack knows it and they know it. Something will make Jason use his knife or not. Since Jack cannot know anything in their heads, he cannot know what will happen next. And he has almost run out of choices himself. He cannot run, not from this position. Or fight. He can still plead, though this has not worked so far. Could he offer them money? After all, that is what this is about, isn't it?

"Listen, please, please, don't, I'll..." His voice thin and cracked. Sounds pathetic.

Jason's face screws up and he lunges towards Jack with a roar. Jack rolls aside, eyes shut. Waits for the pain, feels a jarring of a stone digging into his ribs, holds his breath. A small moan escapes as he hears their laughter. Where is he hit? Where is the pain?

Their voices thread the air, weaving into his head. But he is disappearing, thoughts blurring, the air going black and dancing around him. Is this dying? Is he bleeding away? Why doesn't it hurt? Are his nerves sliced?

Still their laughter, but further away now. Until nothing.

Silence.

CHAPTER 22
SHAME

INTO the silence comes a thought: *This is not silence: I can hear my heartbeat. I am alive.* And into this unexpected idea comes a line from his philosophy revision: *I think; therefore I am.* And in this moment of near death he sees a point to it. *My heart beats; therefore I am.*

Jack begins to pick himself up, bone by bone, carefully, in case he is still bleeding. He looks carefully at the parts of him. Where is it hiding, this terrible injury? But he does not seem to be bleeding. The knife has not touched him. Jason had been teasing him. This makes Jack angry, until he tells himself not to be silly: *If they hadn't been teasing, you'd be dead now. Be thankful for that.*

He stands dazed in the empty street. The moon is behind clouds. The nearest streetlight is some way off. And now Jack begins to shake and his knees feel rubbery. He wraps his arms around his body and holds on to himself. But as the shaking wears off something else takes over: elation. The after-thrill of fear, of risk taken and survived. He wants to laugh or cry. But most of all he wants to run.

First, though, the coin. Suspicion floods through him as he guesses that the men have taken it. Why would they not? He looks around. There is a chance they didn't, if they were only teasing. But he knows this is not likely. And he's right: the coin is not there.

Jack tries to tell himself that it's only a coin, that he can use another one, that nothing will be any different. He knows that this makes sense but this isn't about sense. It's like any so-called lucky coin, or a lucky mascot of any sort. When the mascot is lost or broken, this spells disaster – that's the whole point. It's not that a mascot is valuable in money terms, but it has meaning and power, even if you might not know how it came to be so important. Its power creeps up slowly and from almost nowhere. Jack's coin is like that. And he does not know if he can deal with it because it rattles a part of him which has been holding him together.

Voices. Coming around the corner. Men's voices. Jack begins to run. The fast thud of his feet and the rhythm of his breath are empowering. Faster he runs, the air singing behind him, and soon he is in familiar streets. Thicker grass, big trees, space between houses, sweeter air. His own street. Home. The stone urns with their sea mosses and tiny salt-loving plants. His dad's surfboard against the garage wall. The grass beside the gravel drive. He fumbles for his key and opens the door, shuts it softly behind him and goes into the kitchen. Tea. Biscuits. He's hungry, yes, but mostly he wants to feel familiar things, remind himself that he is alive. So nearly wasn't. Don't think of that now. The kettle sings, the fridge sighs open, the milk glugs, the biscuit crumbles in his mouth and loosens its buttery sugariness. He is home and safe and that should be enough. Lucky Jack, and so nearly not.

Moments later, Jack is walking upstairs, feet sinking into the thick carpet. He shudders when he thinks of the knife, so he stops thinking of it. His father, all this time, has been asleep. He does not know what his son has been through. Would he wish to know? Yes and no. Since he doesn't know, it's best to keep it that way. Their life works well with them both strong.

Jack goes into the bathroom and shuts the door. He runs hot water and scoops it onto his face, again and again, washing away the cold night air, the cats' piss smell of those streets. He catches sight of his face in the mirror and it looks haunted, so he turns away. Cleans his teeth, goes to the toilet, walks into his bedroom and gets undressed. In bed, he pulls the duvet tightly over him and closes his eyes.

But sleep takes a long time to come.

What if is a question that doesn't go away easily.

CHAPTER 23
CRUSHING ROSE PETALS

THE next morning, and Jess arrives at Jack's house. She notices immediately. There is something changed, a darkness about him. His cheek muscles are tight. She notices because she is tuned to him now, noticing everything about him. She would not notice if her mother had spilt egg down her front – as indeed she had that morning – but she would notice a new muscle move in Jack's face. That's the hyperactivity of love.

"You OK?" She breathes the smell of him, feels it go to the hot centre of her when her lips touch his.

"Yeah. Bad night."

A car crunches into the drive: Chris's battered hatchback, with Tommy and Ella. They climb out and all of them go into the garage.

In any band, there are days when the music does not come. This is such a morning. The air is dead. They try, not knowing why it is going wrong. Jack knows. And before long they can see that it comes from him. He is silent, slow, misses entrances, fluffs chords.

Tommy looks at him, his face angry. "What's up with you, Jack?"

"Nothing." Jack shakes his head.

He looks thin, Jess thinks suddenly. She'd never thought he was thin before, but he is. Not weak-looking, for he has muscles on his arms, but the skin over them is fatless. And there are shadows on his face. His T-shirt is baggy and his jeans cover legs that are long and rangy. He looks like a nineteenth-century Romantic poet, she thinks. Full of angst and turmoil. Which is not how she's seen him before. Angst and turmoil are good, though – they push boundaries and Jess knows you have to push boundaries if you want to be free of them.

They return to their playing. They try, really they do. But half an hour later Jack throws down his guitar.

"Shit, this isn't working. Sorry, guys, I need a break." And he hurries from the garage, leaving them staring at each other, the clang of his dropped guitar hanging in the air.

"Stay here," says Jess. And she goes outside. Jack is walking round the back of the house. She follows him. He is hurrying towards a wooden garden seat. Kind of home-made-looking, green with age. It has roses rambling around it. White roses and wine-coloured ones. He sits on it.

"Jack?"

He looks up at her. "Sorry." And he moves along to make space for her.

"What's the matter?

He does not reply except by shrugging his shoulders.

"Can I help?"

Shakes his head.

"Has something happened? You said you had a bad night. I want to help."

"I know you do and I wish you could. But you wouldn't understand."

"Thanks a lot, Jack! You don't know if I wouldn't understand. Try me."

A pause. He could tell her or not tell her. He must surely have that choice. If he doesn't tell her, it will come between them. If he does tell her and she doesn't understand, it will come between them.

"I lost my coin."

She is relieved and is about to say so when she realizes that it must not be so simple. If it was, he would not be like this.

"How? Can we maybe look for it?"

He turns to her and tells her what he did during the night. She feels cold. How could he do this? There is a fear deep inside her that this game is more dangerous even than it seems. But she squashes that fear because she cannot entirely understand it. So, like Jack, she focuses on the coin. She is in love with him and that means absorbing everything about him; it means being sucked in willingly.

Loving isn't about doing what's sensible or right or ordinary, but letting go. Jess wants to understand and agree so much that she will allow her thoughts to be guided in any direction. Even the wrong and dangerous one.

"I thought you said that if you play the game you had to accept everything that happened? I thought that was the whole point? The deal."

He stares at her. "Go on."

She struggles to hold on to what she is going to say. "Well, just that you were going on about making your own luck but luck not coming into it? Luck just being what we call it? How everything has a cause and that if people did tiny things differently then there would be different results. But that you can't ever know what those things would have been. You said you have to make small decisions and go with the consequences. And you said that was what the game was."

"Yes, but now I've lost the coin. The results might be different if I play with another coin."

"Yes, but they might be *better*. Losing the coin and using a different one might be good. Might even be lucky. You won't ever know. But you have to go with it, if you're playing the game, don't you?"

"Yeah."

"Well, seems to me you're not playing the rules of your own game. You've lost the coin, Jack, and maybe that was the price you had to pay. After all, what's a sacrifice if you don't lose something?"

"You may be right. I guess I'm tired. Guess I lost it

there." He sits up. You can tell from his eyes that he is thinking.

Jess speaks. "How about we test a new coin?"

"You got an idea? In particular?"

"The fair. Lots of opportunities to try your theories of chance and luck."

"Excellent! Tonight – let's go tonight." His face is alight now, the thin shadows gone. How easy life can be, she might think if she were thinking. But she's not, just feeling. She smiles too and believes that everything is suddenly all right now.

Lucky Jack. And lucky Jess.

Jack reaches towards her quickly and puts one hand around her neck, pulling her towards him, and their open lips come together. Blood rushes, skin flushes. While they kiss, he reaches for a rose and crushes the petals before sprinkling them on her head and they both melt together. It's very corny but there's nothing new about being in love and no new way of showing it.

Ella calls from the edge of the lawn. "Hey, you two. We've got a band practice, in case you'd forgotten."

"I think perhaps they had," says Tommy. Chris wolf-whistles.

And the rest of the day dissolves in music. The sun blazes down on the garage roof and their sweat fills the closed air. They do not know, any of them, what is happening outside this garage. And even if they could follow the infinite possible movements of myriad particles around the world, they would still be no better at predicting the effects of any of them. If they knew absolutely everything, and the position and state of every atom in the world, they still would not know the future, even if one thing does lead to another.

Because nothing is until it is and until then everything is possible. Which is both scary and also reassuring.

Meanwhile, the fairground awaits Jess and Jack, and fairgrounds contain mysterious darkness. Spirits walk behind the masks and puppets and tricks and deceptions. You can give yourself up to the candyfloss magic in the air and you can laugh with the clowns if you want to. Be careful, though: amongst the fairground lights and their enticing eyes, devils may lurk unseen.

CHAPTER 24
FAIRGROUND ATTRACTION

JACK drags Jess towards the fairground. *Drags* suggests that she is unwilling, but she is not: she has simply almost lost her shoe. She laughs as he pulls her along. She has forgotten his earlier shadowy mood because such things are easily forgotten. In a summer's sweat you cannot remember the feel of sleet.

At night the fairground is a riot of noise and light. Loud and tasteless. Lines of coloured bulbs are looped loosely from every tree, lamppost, fence, caravan, marquee. Rides and stalls are neon-drenched. There goes the giant swing, with a shriek from the passengers as it scoops them skywards. More shrieks from the spinning top and the Ferris wheel.

A man on stilts swallows a glowing sword and the smoke he breathes is red. The crowd *oohs*, though one man shouts that *It's a fake* and *Can't you do it with real fire?* Well, of course it's fake: there's health and safety to consider. Two miniature women are juggling knives – the knives must be plastic but they glint as though they are not – and a queen with no head passes by, dipping her bloody neck towards them.

The music has taken a new tone now that night has fallen. It has darkened, richened, thickened. No longer does it tinkle with childhood games – now is the time when young children are in bed, tucked up, bathed, hair-brushed, kissed and storied. Beneath the grinning puppets, masks and clowns, there is a sinister side to fairs, and when that side begins to walk, small children had better not be there, in case they realize that the clowns are not really laughing.

"Where first?"

"Roller-ghoster?" Jack is pointing to a doorway surrounded by painted ghosts and giant jaws dripping blood. A skinny man dressed as a skeleton is taking money from the small queue.

"Crooked Cottage?" Jess went in this last year: nothing is straight and the senses are disorientated. Harmless fun.

"Toss you for it?"

"So you've chosen a new coin then?"

"Head or tails?" he says, his face doing something impossibly between serious and blue-eyed smiling. His hair is back to its gravity-defying swoops, just as when she first met him. And she knows that really she doesn't care whether it's Roller-ghoster or Crooked Cottage because nothing really matters except being here.

"Tails," she says.

He balances, flicks, spins, catches, covers, slaps and reveals. Grins. "You lose. So, it's definitely my new 'lucky' coin. That proves it."

Jack pulls her towards the Roller-ghoster and they join the queue. He pays the skeleton but pockets his coin carefully. He will not lose it again. Puts his arm around Jess's shoulders and melts inside with the closeness of her.

But wait. This is an important moment. We almost did not notice, as Jack and Jess have not noticed. They have just passed a *what if* moment. *If* the coin had landed the other way and they had gone to the Crooked Cottage, they would not have been waiting outside the Roller–ghoster for two minutes – they'd have been inside the Crooked Cottage, which has no queue and is mostly hidden round another corner. If they'd been inside the cottage, Kelly, Charlie and Samantha and three skinny lads – all six with bottles pretending to be water in their hands – would not have seen them. And events would have turned out differently.

But no one knows this. That's the point. You don't. If you did, it would drive you mad.

Kelly holds her hand up. They stop. It's like a scene from a gangster film. Does she think it's Chicago or something? There she is with her tight white jeans and silly new shoes, her face glossy, lips glistening, nipped waist like Barbie. She is every tacky plastic cliché; she is in many ways ridiculous. You can sneer at her if you want, yet she has a power. And she knows it.

Jack and Jess do not see them. Well, how would they? They are wrapped up in themselves, and everything else recedes into the night air. They are pressed together as Kelly and her friends watch. Samantha starts to speak: "Why, if…"

"Shh," says Kelly. "Let's wait."

And so they wait. They see Jack and Jess go through the entrance to the Roller-ghoster. They do not see what goes on inside, though they can perhaps imagine. Jack and Jess are in the dark, along with a few other people who mean nothing to them, and the screams are of laughter. It's not a frightening ride; it's not meant to be. Fronds of wet stuff brush their faces but they know it's only cloth recently soaked in water and they scream merely because it's cold and wet. Spider webs touch them, of course – how could you have ghosts without spider webs? But they know it's cheap frothy mesh from the market. Plastic skulls glow green and there's a cackling witchy laugh that anyone could do with a bit of practice.

They are sitting in a cart thing and it rattles and shakes their bones, but the track it runs on is hardly of terrifying height. It's all a bit of fun. Not worth the money but no one really cares. It's just one of the things you do, to enter into the spirit of it. And so, very soon, the ride has finished and the cart comes to a rest. One more wet cloth in the face, one more *woooooooo* and they are done.

It's the sort of thing that makes you hungry though. "Fancy a burger?" says Jess. And they walk towards the nearby burger van.

"Don't look round," mutters Jack, as they approach.

She looks, of course. It's them: the Kelly Gang and three skinny lads. Jess's heart sinks and she draws close to Jack, pretending not to see them. It will be no use pretending and they probably know it.

They continue to walk towards the burger van. One customer is in front of them and they stand behind him. Kelly and the others are behind them, talking in silly loud voices.

"Hey, Jack," says Kelly.

He ignores them, though Jess can see his jaw tightening. Jess and Jack catch each other's eyes and smile. They don't feel like smiling. It's a defence mechanism, making out they don't care, even though they do.

"Two burgers please," he says.

"No problem, mate," replies the burger-seller, stirring onions and flipping two burgers that are already sizzling.

"Ignoring me, are you, Jack? Quite right too. Need to keep a better eye on your girlfriend, I'd say. Heard she overdid it on the old booze the other night."

Jess stiffens. Feels her heart racing. Still Jack does not turn round. If he did, he would see Kelly's eyes narrow to slits as she gets no reaction.

"Everyone's talking about it, Jack. Everyone."

"Leave it," whispers Jess, feeling tension in his arms, sensing him take a breath to speak.

"That'll be four-fifty. Help yourselves to ketchup."

Jack hands the money over.

Jess takes her burger. Squirts some ketchup onto it. Puts the roll back together.

Jack begins to do the same.

"Actually," says Kelly, "we've been a bit worried, haven't we, guys?" Mutterings of agreement from her friends, though they don't know what she's talking about. "You see, we heard – 'cos everyone's talking about it... Well, *we* heard that it was drugs. Shouldn't get into stuff like that, you know, Jessica. It can mess with your mind."

Jess will never forget the look on Kelly's face as Jack spins round, ketchup bottle in hand, and a trail of the bright red sauce slices straight down her body, from cheek to thigh.

Kelly gasps, eyes blazing.

"Oh, how careless of me," says Jack, coolly.

"DO something!" screams Kelly. "DO something!"

Samantha turns to the boys with them. The boys are smirking but they soon stop. "What are you waiting for?" she snarls at them. "Are you going to let him get away with that?"

"Run!" says Jack and he pulls Jess with him.

CHAPTER 25
SNAP DECISIONS

THE three skinny lads should have dumped their so-called water bottles instantly. If it had only been water, perhaps they would have. But a few seconds of dithering give Jack and Jess a crucial head start.

Jess and Jack duck into the crowds. Jess is wearing flat shoes but they are flimsy and loose and she would be better off without them. In any case, the one that almost fell off before does so now, and she loses a precious two seconds as she stops to scoop it up. But now she is away, running fast, one-shoed, with Jack pulling her between the people and stalls. They can hear from the noise that their pursuers are close behind them: passers-by shouting angrily – *Oi, you! Mind where you're going! Where's the fire? Hey! Careful, you bloody idiot! Did you see that, Maureen? Really! Freaking kids!*

They cannot know what the lads plan to do when they catch them. Perhaps the lads do not know either. This could be simply three skinny youths chasing a boy and a girl for fun; or it could be very much worse than that. How bad are these boys? They are shouting murderous threats but they may not be serious. Does being skinny make them weak and unused to physical action or does it make them dangerously quick? How dangerous? For all we know, they could be good fighters, brave and cunning, well trained in a martial art, their reflexes honed by boxing lessons or playground tussles or even gang warfare. They could be from violent homes and prison may hold no fears for them.

Or they could simply be three skinny lads who have had a couple of drinks – which will slow them down and impair their judgement – and who happen to have brought knives with them, out of habit. For self defence, they might say, or because they think a knife is the mark of a hard man.

In fact, two of them *are* just skinny lads who've had a few drinks; and the other has indeed had many fights in playgrounds and gangs, some of which he has won and others he has not. And this one does carry a knife and he does think a knife is the sign of a hard man.

If Jack has to face this knife, it will be the second time in two days, which is more times than a decent boy should expect to come across one. But then probability is a weird science and you can easily throw two double sixes in a row, whatever the laws of probability say about it.

The knife-carrier's name is Simon. Which is a nice

enough name and does not suit Simon one bit. For there is very little nice about Simon. Also, if we look more closely at him, we will see that he is not really skinny. He is hard, lean, fat-free. His skin is tight on his body and wiry muscles strain to escape. He is very much stronger than he appears at first. Simon carries the knife because too many people think his small size makes him unthreatening. He is sick of being called skinny, and calling him skinny is something we should not do.

Simon lives on the posh side of town but he spends little time there. His polite parents lost control of him long ago and would be upset but unsurprised to see him now, nasty-faced and furiously chasing a boy and girl through a fairground at night, with a couple of drinks (or more) inside him.

Carrying a knife which did not come from their smart granite kitchen.

Jack and Jess don't know that they are running from a knife but something makes them more afraid the more they run. The chaotic noises around them and pockets of darkness with people dressed strangely begin to work sinister magic. Any forces of good are being sucked from the fairground and replaced by menace. Jack and Jess slide and twist round corners, dodging jesters and a man dressed as a tiger, throngs of people, huge stilted giants, acrobats, candyfloss-sellers, everything a blur. Screams from rides, cries from hawkers, bangs of fireworks and fake shooting galleries, all jumbled. A man grabs Jack, thinking that he is running because he has committed a crime, and Jess shouts in fear. "No!" Jack wriggles free and the man is left behind.

Though they can't look round, they sense that not all three boys are following them now. They are right. One has stopped, spitting and retching after the unusual exercise. Another is lagging some way behind Simon. Only Simon still follows close. And he is very close. In fact, he could probably reach them within seconds if he pushed himself, but he is waiting his moment. His mind keeps coming back to the knife still strapped to his wrist. It is warm and it makes him feel strong every time he senses it. He can afford to wait for the right moment.

Jess's breath comes in shallow gasps now. She is not used to this. It hurts. Her bare foot slips on the grass. Her throat rasps and stings, her chest stabs, her head feels hot. She knows she is slowing down.

"Let's stop. Please."

"Can't let him win. Come on!" urges Jack beside her, dragging her arm.

"Can't. Go on. Much longer." She knows. And yes, she's a bit scared of stopping and facing her pursuers, but not *that* scared. Though she should be.

Still they run, though there is hesitation in Jack now. After all, what is the worst that can happen?

The circus show will begin soon and criers are rounding up the crowds. Movement is in one direction, with Jack and Jess going against the flow. They are coming to a quieter part of the fairground now, away from the noisiest rides and stalls. They need the crowds.

Jess is past thinking or caring but Jack's mind is alert – *Must get back to the crowds. Could hide in crowds.*

During the chase there have been many choices of lefts and rights, and Jack has made those choices too quickly to think. Thanks to those snap decisions – and many other things leading to them: spinning the new coin, going in the Roller-ghoster, choosing to go to the fair at all – the chase ends where it does and in the way it does.

A noise behind them. A curse and a yell. Simon slips on wet mud. It gives them valuable seconds.

Jack and Jess run faster.

Gaining ground.

A turn, then another, doubling back. Have they lost him? Slipping behind some caravans, dodging, leaping over and round buckets and boxes and rubbish. Tangled rope. Flapping newspaper. Plastic bags. A Mexican hat.

And here they are, gasping for breath, face to face with Simon, who stands there, triumphant. Hot-faced they all are, staring at each other.

Just here.

Just behind the fortune-teller's caravan.

Fantastic Farantella the Famous Fairground Fortune-teller – Your Future Foretold for a Fiver – She Can See It Coming! Mind you, Jack and Jess can't see the front of the caravan, as they are hiding behind it.

"So what are you going to do now, then?" asks Jack.

"I think you're going to come with me, so's you can say sorry to Kelly."

"You going to make us?"

"Yep."

"Look, just go back to your owner, why don't you?" says Jack, trying to sound bored. "She deserved all she got. She even deserves you. Come on, Jess, we're out of here."

"Oh no, I don't think so." A voice behind them.

Jack and Jess turn. One of the other lads is standing behind them. No wonder Simon seems so relaxed. "Meet Joe," says Simon. They turn to Simon again. He is closing in and his eyes are nasty. And there's a knife in his hand. Jess feels sick instantly.

It is strange what the mind is drawn to in times like this and Jack finds himself thinking of the coin in his pocket. He needs to keep it safe. He feels that if he can keep the coin safe then all will be well. It is an illogical thought but it is the only one he has. He does not look at the knife.

Jess is about to say something.

From behind them comes Joe's voice. "Security. Coming this way."

CHAPTER 26
FANTASTIC FARANTELLA

SIMON'S face shrivels in anger. "Catch you later, jerks, but trust me: you will apologize to Kelly, or you'll be sorry." And he walks away, the knife hidden. Joe goes in the other direction. They must be practised at walking away from trouble pretending to be innocent because, actually, they do a good job, Jess thinks: they saunter, hands in pockets.

The security men haven't seen them yet. One of them begins to speak into a radio. It is impossible to be sure whether they are even looking for Simon or if they are simply there by chance.

"Let's get out of here," says Jack. He holds her hand as they slip round the side of the caravan. Of course, in theory, Jack and Jess have nothing to fear, as they are innocent as far as the law is concerned, but they do not want to be involved. Jack's mind races ahead to possible questions and then being blamed by Simon and his cronies if they get them into trouble. Peering round from behind the caravan again, Jack and Jess watch Simon and Joe slip around a corner of another vehicle and the security men walk in the wrong direction.

At any moment, Simon will turn his attention back to Jack and Jess.

"Quick!" whispers Jess. "In here." Fantastic Farantella's door is open, draped in a thick red velvet curtain. There's a handwritten sign, which has fallen on the floor: *Open for future business. Come in – I've been expecting you.* A crystal ball straight out of Pound 4 All sits beside it, trying to sparkle with its cheap glitter covering.

Simon is turning, peering. Joe is with him. At any moment…

Jess pulls Jack through the doorway. Several layers of red velvet close behind them and they are in near darkness. A tall woman has been on the phone and she jumps to her feet, startled.

"Blimey, give me some warning, why don't you?"

Jess manages to stop herself from saying, *Sorry, we thought you could see the future.* Jack knows what she's thinking and they both feel laughter welling up.

"Look, I'm on a break," says Fantastic Farantella. "I'm not supposed to be on again for another half-hour. Can't you read the sign?"

"Sorry – but it said open. Really, it did," says Jack politely.

"We're very sorry." Jess uses her wide eyes and the most innocent voice she can find.

Farantella sniffs. "Well, you'll have to go. I need a break. Knackered, I am."

"Look, please," says Jess. "You see, I've always wanted my fortune told and I've heard you're the best." She puts her shoe back on.

"Yes," says Jack, "Everyone says so. And this is the only day we can come and…"

"We've been saving up. Please."

Farantella is not impressed and she is not a kind woman. But she could do with the money. It's not easy earning a living as a fortune-teller in the age of science, when no one believes in fate and destiny any more. Not that she does either, but it's always paid the bills. And sometimes, especially after a shot of whisky, she really does get visions and vibes when she touches people, so who knows? The scientists haven't explained everything, after all. And long may that continue, as far as Farantella is concerned.

She sniffs again. "Oh, all right, but you won't mind if I drink my tea while I'm doing it?"

They shake their heads.

"And it'll be ten quid."

"It says a fiver."

"There's two of you, love. They not teach you maths at school?" Catch Farantella on a good day and she'll let you in for a reduced price, but this isn't a good day. Mind you, they're nice enough kids, nothing wrong with them that she can see, and the boy has cute eyes – though weird hair. To be honest, she needs a fag but she's trying to give up. She's at that fidgety-fingered stage. If they push her too far, she'll maybe give them something to worry about in the fortune she tells them. One of those *Oh no, I see horror! Oh, horrible things; Oh you poor dear – take care now!* Mind you, you're not allowed to do that these days, what with the regulations. It's many years since Farantella disliked someone enough to predict a nasty accident. Besides, it frightens off the punters. And she'd once heard a story that a fairground fortune-teller had been caught up in some legal case when a punter had accused her of causing post-traumatic stress disorder. Farantella can do without that.

"We haven't got ten quid, have we?" Jack turns to Jess, innocent-eyed.

Jess shakes her head. Outside they can hear shouting. It might be Simon and Joe or the security men or someone completely different. Farantella sees her looking, cocks her head. "You being chased then? That why you arrived in such a hurry?"

"Please, you could do us a really quick fortune-telling – maybe we could find seven-fifty? Please. And we'll tell everyone about you."

Farantella could do with seven-fifty for a few minutes of making stuff up.

"Eight quid. But I do you together, mind."

"Done." Jack and Jess pool their money. Not including the lucky coin, of course.

"OK," says Fantastic Farantella the Famous Fairground

Fortune-teller. "Now, just a minute. I'm not quite ready, what with you crashing in on me like that."

She gets some matches, lights a few incense sticks, takes a swig of her tea, and presses the button on a CD player. Watery whale music drifts out. She pokes a head and arm through the curtained doorway and rights the sign so that it really does say "Closed". They hear her shouting, "Oi, what you doing hanging about? I'm closed." And she comes back in, scowling.

Farantella sits down at the table and signals to them to sit, beckoning with a swooping, dramatic arm. She slowly drapes something like a piece of net curtain over her head and pulls a crystal ball from under the table, sets it on a saucer covered in crumpled tin foil and finds the plastic switch on the side. The ball starts to moan and glow. Jess feels Jack begin to shake with laughter and she refuses to look at him.

Fantastic Farantella closes her eyes. A hum comes from her nose, vibrating. It goes on for a long time, but then Farantella starts coughing. She takes a slug of tea. Opens her eyes.

Stares at them both. They stare back, wide-eyed, every muscle frozen to trap the laughter. "You are drawn together," she says, in a drony voice. "Am I right?"

They nod. Well, it's hardly rocket science. She'll need to do better than that.

Farantella's hands are hovering above the crystal ball. It stops moaning, begins buzzing and then the light goes off.

"Bugger," says Farantella. "I knew that was going to happen."

Laughter explodes from Jack's nose and Jess gulps. Hysteria is rising in her. Farantella reaches in a drawer, finds a new battery and inserts it into a slot beneath the ball, all with the net curtain still on her head. The ball lights up again and continues its moaning. The smoky incense dries the air and Farantella inhales deeply.

She closes her eyes. "Close your eyes," she snaps. They do. "Breathe deeply and relax – otherwise how can I read your fortunes?" They try. Farantella tries not to think of her next cigarette – because she knows she's going to have one, just one, as soon as these kids have gone. But she's taken money from them, so she'd better give them something or they'll probably have trading standards on to her and it wouldn't be the first visit she's had from the men with clipboards. *Calm yourself, Doreen.* (Doreen is her real name but Doreen the Fortune-teller does not have the same ring.) But her mind has gone blank. She should have had that tea and a biscuit before expecting the muse to be with her. "Give me a hand, both of you." Perhaps she will get some inspiration from touching them. And she holds out her own, soon feeling Jack and Jess put a hand in each of hers.

Still nothing. "Hmm, strange. I must be tired. I'm getting nothing." She doesn't think it's strange, just annoying. Where is her inspiration, her creativity, when she needs it? She doesn't expect to see the future, not really, but a few visionary vibes wouldn't go amiss.

It's not much to ask, is it, for a fortune-teller of her experience?

"What do you mean, nothing?"

"No vibes, love. Dead, your hands are."

"That's creepy. What are you saying?"

Farantella grins and waves her hands at them, making childish ghostly noises. "Wooooooooooo!" And then she laughs. "No, I'm being silly – I just mean I haven't tuned in yet. Tuning in's hard, you know. I have to be in the right mood."

"Look, maybe you can just give us our money back," says Jack. "It's fine, we understand."

"It's a shame though," says Jess. "I was looking forward to that."

"Yeah, well," says Jack. "It's all a bit of a joke really, though, isn't it?"

"Excuse me, mate," says Fantastic Farantella. "Who're you calling a joke? I was telling fortunes while you were still dribbling milk and I have had some spectacular successes. Spectacular. Not my fault if you've put up a psychic barrier and it's a little harder for me to get through to the other side, is it? OK, right, I've got an idea. Give me something that's close to you."

"But we've already given you money."

"No, stupid, I'm not going to keep it. I need to hold something, from each of you, together. Something that you keep close to you, that has your heart in it, bit of your soul. I need to hold a bit of your soul in my hand." And she grins.

"I've got this necklace," says Jess. And she takes a thin silver chain from her neck.

"Just the ticket. And you?"

Jack brings the coin, the lucky coin, from his pocket.

"That's not very impressive," says Farantella. "You need emotional attachment, you know."

"This is a special coin," says Jack, and he spins it into the air, catching it in a way that makes it seem drawn to his hand.

"If you say so," says Farantella, thinking of the cigarette she craves more and more. "Anyway, give it here." And she takes the necklace and winds it round the coin and then encloses them in her hands.

Jess and Jack watch carefully, thinking she may have a secret talent for disappearing tricks even if she's rubbish at telling fortunes.

For a few long moments the scene goes still. We can look down on them and see the dark red room with the tacky glowing crystal ball moaning away on its new battery. There's the incense swirling, the mug of tea, Farantella with her net curtain. The distant sounds of the fairground are still outside and we have no idea where Simon and Joe are but we don't have to worry about them just now. There's a Post-it note reminding Farantella that she has a dentist's appointment tomorrow.

And into this unlikely setting, a sinister spirit enters. If we believe in such things. Or if we don't, then something else we can't rightly explain. Jess shivers. Jack finds her hand. For some reason, they do not feel like laughing now. Both of them stare at Farantella. Her eyes are screwed shut but suddenly across her face flies something that clutches at her, twisting the muscles of her mouth. She bends forward quickly, her shoulders hunching.

A small noise slips from her mouth. Or the noise could come from somewhere else – it is hard to say. It is the noise a spirit would make. If such things existed. It is the noise that the future would make, if it squeezed through a gap in the skin of time.

CHAPTER 27
FORTUNE OR FAKE

JACK and Jess. Struggling in their minds. Clawing reality back. Their heads tell them that this is fake, or has an ordinary explanation – perhaps that Farantella is ill or messing around with them. She is a charlatan – how could she be anything else, with her plastic ball, dud battery, mug of tea, grubby veil from some old granny's suburban bungalow window? Besides, no one really believes this stuff.

And yet. And yet. There are things beyond explanation. Science cannot tell us everything. Perhaps something beyond the natural world has indeed entered this caravan and this fortune-teller's mind.

Otherwise, why would Jack and Jess have shivered so soon after laughing? Why both of them? For they both feel it: that there is something heavy in the caravan, something thickening the air, a chill breath of strangeness.

Farantella's eyes are still closed. She is gripping the crystal ball as though trying to crush it. And she is shaking her head.

This is, surely, an act. It is absurd. Jack and Jess should be laughing. This is like some ancient music-hall act, or a scene from a very bad horror film.

But Jess and Jack are right not to laugh. For this is not, in fact, an act. Farantella is not making this up. This is real. Though it has nothing to do with the plastic ball or what she may or may not see in it while her eyes are shut.

Farantella has a severe pain in her guts. That's all. Maybe it was something she ate – she should get health and safety on to that dodgy burger guy who never washes his hands. Maybe it's been too much strong tea and desperately needing a fag and it's all just turned her bowels to water. Whichever, Farantella doesn't need to be a fortune-teller to know she needs these kids to go. Quickly.

There is always the possibility, of course, that there really is a spirit in the room and that this has turned her insides to liquid. Maybe that's why she says what she does.

The words just come from her mouth. She feels them coming, senses them make their way towards her lips, but she does not know where they come from. It's times like this when she has had her spectacular successes in the past – something in the air simply enters her. She's never tried to explain it. Actually, we should be a bit scientific about this – there have been other times when she's been moved by what *felt* like a spirit, just like this, and yet she's got it totally wrong, but Farantella conveniently forgets these times. After all, what would it do to her confidence if she thought she was wrong as often as right? And confidence is important when you're selling the future.

Anyway, for whatever reason, words slip from her mouth.

"Red, I see red. Red things. Red for danger. And boats. I think they're boats. Maybe not, could be something else in the water. Big things. Sharks? Whales? Something beginning with 'w'. Wings. Yes, I see wings. Are you flying somewhere? Going on a journey? Beware of wings. And water. And whales, or something in the water. Soon."

Farantella pushes her chair back. She needs them to go now. What she's said has startled her. But she cares very little, is really hardly thinking about it. She just needs them to go. That pain in her guts: it's taking her breath away.

"That's it. You've had your time. Close the curtain behind you." She hands back the coin and necklace.

Her forehead is creased, her skin grey, her eyes dull. She bustles around, switching off the plastic ball, stubbing out the incense sticks. Jack and Jess stand up. They feel cold.

Farantella is obviously not going to say anything else, so they leave, mumbling hasty thanks, though they have no idea what for. It doesn't seem like a very good way to spend eight pounds. And yet, they got what they came for: refuge from Simon, and a pretty good act by a weird fortune-teller. What did they expect? Truth?

Outside, they hurry away, looking around carefully for any sign of Simon and co. Nothing. They slip through the glitter of the fairground, enveloping themselves in the noise and light. But there is nothing more for them here and they make their way home, Jack accompanying Jess to hers first.

It is very dark as they walk towards her house. The sky is moonless, starless. A thin wind chills the sweat on their skin and they hold each other tight as they walk, their bodies fitting together as though designed to do so.

Ghosts follow them, traces of the fear and strangeness they had felt in that caravan. They must shrug the spirits away or they may be taken over by them. And so they laugh, at first with difficulty but then more loudly. *Red things! Big things! Wings or whales or something beginning with "w"! Weather? What if it rains – wooooo, beware the wind, Jack! Oh and walls, dangerous things: walls. Especially when in water. Witches, obviously. Werewolves. Wine. Windows. Walnuts – well, you could be allergic, or choke on one. Warlocks and wizards. Weasels. Wine gums. Worms. Wardrobes. Watering cans.*

And by the time Jack and Jess kiss at Jess's garden gate, they have forgotten that there was anything to fear.

Soon, but not very soon, disentangled but still with the blush of him hot on her skin, Jess goes into her house and smiles goodbye to Jack standing there watching her.

Sylvia is in the kitchen. She is trying to clear up broken glass with kitchen paper. There is blood on the kitchen paper. And on the floor. Not much – this is not a medical emergency – but there is no doubt that if Sylvia was sober she would have been using something sensible to sweep up the broken glass. And, in fact, the glass would not have been broken.

"What are you doing, Mum?"

"What does it look like I'm doing?"

"How did that happen?"

"Your father phoned again."

"And you broke a glass."

"Accident."

"What did he say?"

"You didn't email him. You said you would. If you'd emailed when you said, he wouldn't have phoned and then I wouldn't have broken the glass."

"I haven't had time." Though Jess knows she has. She just hasn't thought about it. But it's unreasonable for her mum to blame the broken glass on her when she wasn't even there.

Sylvia is not being effective with the kitchen paper. Normally – previously – Jess would have taken over, helped her. But she can still taste Jack on her lips and she wants to keep that with her rather than being jerked into the ugly reality of a mother wiping gin from the kitchen floor and blaming an absent father rather than her own weakness.

Jess is, in short, irritated.

And for this small spiteful reason she will not email her father that night either. She will wait till the morning. Just because. Now, she will go up to her room and think of Jack and music and dreams of freedom.

Her mother can sort herself out. Jess hands her the dustpan and brush and goes up the stairs, blocking it all out. It is a moment when the crack between them widens. And yet that is necessary and right in many ways.

The trouble is: sending the email the next morning instead of now may turn out to be very important, or it may not. Jess will never know. But we will, because we can see more. We can see glimpses of worlds that do not happen as well as those that do.

For we have reached one of those knife-edge *what if* moments again. Where lives will go one way or another spinning on a tiny difference. Here are two possibilities. Only one will actually happen. We will look at them both and then play Jack's Game and let the coin decide.

NOTE:

Only one of the next two chapters will happen. A coin will spin and the story will follow whichever event the coin "decides".

CHAPTER 28
HEADS

JESS'S father is driving a bright-red hired car. Fast. He probably shouldn't be driving, as he's still somewhat jet-lagged from his late flight the night before. A restless night in an airport hotel and now he's heading towards London, where he'll be staying in a decent establishment, courtesy of the university, which has sent him on an extended trip across the Atlantic. Then a week of meetings and lectures before he'll travel to see his daughter. Still hasn't had an email from her, which is annoying, and that phone call with Sylvia set his teeth on edge. She sounded even more fragile than ever.

Funny, he'd loved her for that once, but fragility can become very boring. She'd only been twenty-one when they'd married and twenty-three when Jessica had been born, but by the time she was thirty he'd really wanted to tell her, *Grow up, for crying out loud.* Let's face it: they were too different. And he'd partly fallen for her to annoy his own family, who wanted him to marry a good Italian Catholic girl. That was unfair of him; but he'd been young too. He'd stayed with her till Jessica was ten and then the big academic job in Chicago had been a good excuse. He'd gone, and had never once regretted it. Best thing for Sylvia too, probably. And his second wife is nothing like her: strong, career-minded, icicle-focused, but with Italian passion. Perfect. Or as perfect as you could hope for.

At least Jessica isn't like her mother either. Head on her shoulders, that one. Though she should have emailed him as he'd asked. Probably Sylvia didn't pass the message on. Lorenzo loves his daughter, though he may not have much opportunity to show it. He doesn't see that as his fault. Life.

He wonders if Jessica is still talking about music college. She'd mentioned it months ago and he's been waiting for her to ask again – when he'd reminded her, she'd kind of clammed up, said she didn't think it was such a good idea any more. He's planning to ask her and offer to pay for it. Though she must have missed the deadline for this year now. Mind you, he'll have to get past the barbed-wire fence of Sylvia's hang-ups first. But he'll cross that bridge, etc.

Lorenzo yawns. Looks at the clock: 10.52. His eyes are prickly with tiredness. He needs coffee. He'll stop at some town near the motorway – not one of those awful service stations full of ugly fat Brits in cheap clothes – and have something quick to eat and drink.

Roughly half an hour later, he parks in a car park in a decent town. Gets out and locks the door. Lorenzo appreciates good cars and this is not a good one. He likes the colour – loud, rich red – but it wasn't a model he was comfortable being seen in. And the girl at the hire-car place had not been very helpful.

Anyway. Having that argument had held him up, delayed him by a quarter of an hour while the girl phoned around to see if there was a better car available. There wasn't, so he had the red one.

Irritating. Sylvia always said he let small things get to him. Well, he isn't about to change now. Or ever. He is quite happy with the way he is.

A couple of possible coffee places are closed for Sunday but he finds a small upmarket establishment along the street. It's 11.24 when he arrives. Soon he is drinking a coffee and eating a panini. Or, he is *trying* to eat it but it really is absurdly hot. Why can't they make them a sensible temperature? He sips his coffee. Also too hot. His phone is on the table in front of him. He keeps glancing at it, hoping for an email from Jessica. If she doesn't contact him soon he'll email her. He needs to know which day she can see him – he'll have to tell the hotel; and find somewhere to stay when he sees her.

He looks around. Two women are talking too loudly. An overweight mother feeds chocolate cake to an overweight child. The father (or maybe an unconnected man) reads a Sunday paper. A young man and woman stare into each other's eyes and the man touches the tip of her nose with some cappuccino froth. Lorenzo looks away.

Tries another mouthful of his panini, which is just about bearable at the edges. More coffee. Still too hot. Really feels the need of a decent caffeine kick. Should have asked for a double shot.

Glances at the mobile again. Nothing. Picks it up. He will email her. In a moment. Drums his fingers. Takes another slug of coffee. Taps the phone to open up a new email screen. It's 11.45, he notices, because time is something which is important to him.

Thinks. What best to say? Doesn't want to sound as though he's nagging. He'd like this visit to be just right. After all, it's not often your only daughter leaves school. He deserves to be part of that, doesn't he? He's not a bad father – they were just a bad couple and it's best for everyone that they are not together. Maybe he'll arrange to send flowers. Would that be a nice touch? Or not. Probably not.

He taps in the letters:

Dear Jessica, Hope your mother told you I'd phoned. Need to know about the weekend. Email me asap please. Dadx

The clock digits slip to 11.47.

And behind him the window explodes. Shatters. Noise. Glass. Screaming. Something flying through the air. Chairs scraped back. More screaming. Glass on his table, on his lap. Blood oozes from his hand. It doesn't hurt. Some people are running; others sitting with shocked faces, brushing glass away. There's so much noise that he can't hear anything. Can make no sense. Time does something weird. He thinks it's a bomb. Or gas. Can he smell it? Suddenly he can. But a woman is laughing. You don't laugh when a bomb goes off. Do you? Also, no one seems dead. Other people have glass on their tables, but he seems to be the only one who is bleeding. It still doesn't hurt. There's glass on his panini, in his coffee. All these things he takes in, one by one and at the same time. It's that sort of weirdness.

His legs don't move. Won't. He isn't sure he's trying, can't remember what it is you do when you want your legs to move.

And then he understands.

A pigeon. That's all. Smashed right through the window. The bird is flapping horribly among the cups and saucers and plates and bottles of syrup and canisters of chocolate powder. There is blood on its head and one wing doesn't seem quite right.

A load of girls at the back of the coffee shop are screaming. One member of staff has her apron over her head. The manager is attempting to take control. But it is, frankly, chaos. And Lorenzo wants out of it. It is not his problem and there is nothing he can do to help. His brain engages and now he can move his legs. He stands up, brushing glass from his clothes, picks up his phone and leaves. 11.50, the phone says.

His heart is racing but on the surface he seems calm. Outside, he looks back at the empty area of the window. The hole is oddly symmetrical and almost circular. He'd never have thought a broken window would look like that – if he'd had to imagine it, it would have had jagged edges. Mind you, he'd never have expected a pigeon to smash through a window. Just shows you how unexpected the world can be. He shakes his head to rid himself of peculiar thoughts, get himself back to the logical, controlled person that he is. A coupled of shards of glass tinkle to the ground.

The bird lurches with drunken wings across a table. A waiter scoops it up with a tea towel and then doesn't know what to do with it. A customer strokes its head. Lorenzo can't hear what they're saying. Anyway, it's just a bird. But no doubt they'll take it to the vet or call the RSPCA or something.

Customers stand in huddles, talking loudly about how amazing it was that a bird flew through the window. At the very least they should get a free meal out of it, they joke. Or not joke. Their faces are all lit up.

Lorenzo finds their reactions irritating. The screaming and then the chitchat, as though this is about the most interesting thing that's ever happened to them. All he'd wanted was a quiet, quick coffee and snack. He'd paid for it too. Should have got a refund, but that would have taken longer. A snarl of anger increases his hunger.

Lorenzo goes back to the car. He contemplates getting a coffee from somewhere else, but he can't see anywhere near by and he decides not to. Better just to get going. The tiny cut on his hand has stopped bleeding.

Then he remembers: he hasn't sent the email. He opens it up again. Clicks SEND, though his last thought as he does so is that it's a little abrupt, could have been more friendly. Never mind. She should have emailed him. Then he wouldn't have had to nag.

11.55.

His heart is still racing as he drives off. The car pulls on to the main road, and before long joins the dual carriageway. And the motorway. He has a slight headache now. Combination of jet lag, low blood sugar from hunger, and physical shock. Perhaps he should have got coffee from somewhere else. Maybe he should stop at a service station after all. He rubs his eyes.

It is worth noticing – though Lorenzo is not thinking of this – that if it was not for the pigeon, he would have been at this particular section of motorway a bit later. Also, his concentration would be better – thanks to a combination of coffee, food and the lack of both stress and preoccupation about the exploding window. It takes a while for a shock like that to subside.

Then there is, or will be, Jess's email, which will arrive as he's driving, if Jess remembers to send it.

The email that Jess should have sent the night before. And would have done if her drunken mother had not annoyed her by breaking a glass in the kitchen.

12.04.

Also, if the hire-car company had given him the car he'd wanted in the first place, instead of this red one, he'd have been at this spot at a slightly different time.

Mind you, the same could be said if he'd left five minutes later, or earlier.

Not to mention that it's a red car. Red. Not that that should make any difference at all, surely. Farantella saying beware of red was just a coincidence, *obviously*. We must not fall into the trap of believing that this is relevant at all. Red cars are supposed to have more accidents anyway, so there's even some science going on here.

But there's something else we don't know about yet: a car driven by an idiot is speeding towards a junction rather close to where Jess's father happens to be. What will happen next depends on exactly where Jess's father is at exactly what time and on his ability to react if Jess's email arrives at just the wrong moment.

12.06.

In order to know for certain what might happen, we would need to be able to predict the position of every particle. But the tiniest unimaginable particles may change when observed, so just by *watching* Jess's father and the idiot and all the other cars on the road, and the pigeon, we could be changing the future. It's that scary.

The red car is spinning along. Lorenzo's thoughts are with the exploding window and the flapping pigeon and people laughing and screaming. His headache is a little worse. He takes a hand from the steering wheel and squeezes the place between his eyes. It helps for a few seconds but as soon as he takes his fingers away, the throb returns.

The phone sits on the passenger seat beside him. He glances at it. Nothing.

12.07.

Idiot is on the slip road, coming on to the motorway. He doesn't want to wait. Black car in the left lane needs to do something – speed up? Slow down? Move to the right? Can't speed up: there's a car in front. Can't slow down: there's a car behind. Too many cars everywhere – people going shopping.

Idiot is not slowing down.

12.08.

Black car needs to move into overtaking lane.

Lorenzo, foot on brake, slows.

Black car swerves. In front of him.

Close.

Very close.

Frowns. Heart skittering. Cars dancing. Grips the steering wheel. Creases forehead. Ache. Eyes blurry. He blinks.

Idiot slices on to the motorway. Lorenzo scowls at him. A horn blares. Idiot grins. *What's your problem, mate?*

The phone.

Bleeps.

An email.

He glances down.

12.08.

Back to the road. Back to the screen. It's Jess. Horns blare. Foot on brakes. Cars in front. *What?* Idiot – in front of black car. Red lights.

Braking.
Skidding.
Swerving.
Screeching.
Screaming.
Burning.
Black.

The phone flies through the air as the windscreen shatters.

Jess's father has gone.

12.08.

CHAPTER 29
TAILS

JESS'S father is driving a silver car. Fast. He probably shouldn't be driving, as he's still somewhat jet-lagged from his late flight the night before. A restless night in an airport hotel and now he's heading towards London, where he'll be staying in a decent establishment, courtesy of the university, which has sent him on an extended trip across the Atlantic. Then a week of meetings and lectures before he'll travel to see his daughter. Still hasn't had an email from her, which is annoying, and that phone call with Sylvia set his teeth on edge. She sounded even more fragile than ever.

Funny, he'd loved her for that once, but fragility can become very boring. She'd only been twenty-one when they'd married and twenty-three when Jessica had been born, but by the time she was thirty he'd really wanted to tell her, *Grow up, for crying out loud.* Let's face it: they were too different. And he'd partly fallen for her to annoy his own family, who wanted him to marry a good Italian Catholic girl. That was unfair of him; but he'd been young too. He'd stayed with her till Jessica was ten and then the big academic job in Chicago had been a good excuse. He'd gone, and had never regretted it once. Best thing for Sylvia too, probably. And his second wife is nothing like her: strong, career-minded, icicle-focused, but with Italian passion. Perfect. Or as perfect as you could hope for.

At least Jessica isn't like her mother either. Head on her shoulders, that one. Though she should have emailed him as he'd asked. Probably Sylvia didn't pass the message on. Lorenzo loves his daughter, though he may not have much opportunity to show it. He doesn't see that as his fault. Life.

He wonders if Jessica is still talking about music college. She'd mentioned it months ago and he's been waiting for her to ask again – when he'd reminded her, she'd kind of clammed up, said she didn't think it was such a good idea any more. He's planning to ask her and offer to pay for it. Though she must have missed the deadline for this year now. Mind you, he'll have to get past the barbed-wire fence of Sylvia's hang-ups first. But he'll cross that bridge, etc.

Lorenzo's mind empties, freewheels for a while.

He soon yawns. Looks at the clock: 10.43. His eyes are prickly with tiredness. He needs coffee. He'll stop at some town near the motorway – not one of those awful service stations full of ugly fat Brits in cheap clothes – and have something quick to eat and drink.

Less than half an hour later, he parks in a car park in a decent town. Gets out and locks the door. Lorenzo appreciates good cars and this is a good one.

A couple of possible coffee places are closed for Sunday but he finds a small upmarket establishment along the street. It's 11.09 when he arrives. Soon Lorenzo sits drinking his coffee and eating a panini, which is just the right temperature. He sips his coffee. His phone is on the table in front of him. He keeps glancing at it, hoping for an email from Jessica. If she doesn't contact him soon he'll email her. He needs to know which day she can see him – he'll have to tell the hotel; and find somewhere to stay when he sees her.

He looks around. Three teenagers huddle round a laptop discussing something. An overweight woman has just arrived and is taking an overweight baby out of its pushchair, while simultaneously ordering chocolate cake. Two women enter, talking in loud voices as they open the door. A man reads a Sunday newspaper. A young man and woman stare into each other's eyes and she touches the tip of his nose with some cappuccino froth. Lorenzo looks away.

Nearly finished his panini. Coffee almost gone. Really needs a bigger caffeine kick. Should have asked for a double shot. He looks at his watch: 11.30 – plenty of time. Maybe he'll get a quick espresso.

Glances at the mobile again. Nothing. Picks it up.

He will email her. In a moment. Drums his fingers. Takes another slug of coffee. Taps the phone to open up a new email screen. It's 11.32, he notices, because time is something which is important to him.

Thinks. What best to say? Doesn't want to sound as though he's nagging. He'd like this visit to be just right. After all, it's not often your only daughter leaves school. He deserves to be part of that, doesn't he? He's not a bad father – they were just a bad couple and it's best for everyone this way. Maybe he'll arrange for flowers to be sent. Would that be a nice touch?

He taps in the letters:

Dear Jessica, Hope your mother told you I'd phoned. Need to know about the weekend. Email me asap please. Dadx

Reads it back. No, too abrupt. He starts again.

Hi, Jessica,

Hope your mother told you I'd phoned. Really looking forward to seeing you soon. But I need to know (asap) which day would be better. I know you've got your prom so Saturday won't work, your mother says. Sunday? Monday? I need to let my hotel know. Maybe we could go for a meal. And I've got a present for you!

Must go. On my way to London now. Email me asap please.

Much love, Dadxx

Lorenzo touches the screen to send it. 11.36. Orders an espresso and downs it quickly, finishes his panini, leaves a tip and goes back to the car. He wants to get going now.

11.38.

The car pulls on to the main road, and soon joins the dual carriageway. And the motorway. He still doesn't feel entirely recovered from the flight, but the coffee and food have certainly helped. He rubs his eyes to remove traces of a slight headache.

Roughly twenty minutes later, a car driven by an idiot is speeding towards a slip road on to the motorway, but that is several miles behind where Jess's father is by this time, so should not affect him. We can watch it though, since we are here.

The car driven by the idiot is on the slip road, coming on to the motorway. The idiot doesn't want to wait. Black car in the left lane needs to do something – speed up? Slow down? Move to the right? Can't speed up: there's a car in front. Can't slow down: there's a car behind. Too many cars everywhere – people going shopping.

Idiot is not slowing down.

Black car needs to move into overtaking lane. No choice. It slips into a dangerously small space. Horns tear the air.

Hearts skitter. Cars dance. Drivers scowl, mouths open, angry. Lights flash. Feet on brakes. Fingers squeeze steering wheels. Breathing freezes.

The idiot slices on to the motorway. A horn blares. Idiot grins. *What's your problem, mate?*

Heads shake. Eyes ahead. Lucky escape. For everyone. Could have been so much worse.

12.07.

If...

Meanwhile, some miles ahead, Lorenzo is driving fast. He wants to get to London before the traffic gets worse. He's looking forward to being in his hotel, having his first glass of chilled white wine. Fancies some decent city food. Classy surroundings. On expenses.

He's in control, which is where he likes to be. He's not in control of everyone else on the road though. And some people drive like idiots.

The phone.

Bleeps.

An email.

He glances down.

12.08.

Back to the road. Then back to the screen again. It's Jess. He slides a hand onto the phone, touches the icon. He knows you're not supposed to read texts and things while driving, but he won't pick it up, just glance down. He's not an idiot. Wouldn't put himself in danger. Or not deliberately. No one *wants* to have an accident, after all, but it's only stupid people who can't control a phone with their left hand and the steering wheel with their right.

Glances down. He's touched the wrong bit of the screen. Tries again. The email opens.

Hi, Dad, Mum said you ...

Back to the road.

... phoned. Sorry I ...

The car in front of him is slowing, for some reason.

... didn't email you last ...

Traffic is thickening ahead. Roadworks, maybe.

... night. Really ...

Lorenzo slows a little. Keeps his place. He's a good driver.

... busy – I'm singing ...

But now the car behind is too close. Way too close.

... with the band that's ...

He gestures angrily with his hand. *God, there are maniacs on the road!*

... playing at the prom ...

A lorry in the middle lane is overtaking another. Racing, by the look of it. Stupid. Lorries can't do that on hills. Everything else is slowing, cars all too close. If anyone makes a mistake now...

He needs to scroll the screen. Feels with his fingers. Strokes it.

Looks down.

Car in front speeds up. Lorenzo too. Foot on accelerator. Passing the lorries now.

Both hands on steering wheel. Presses horn angrily as he passes.

Lorry driver laughing. One finger in the air.

Idiot.

so can't see you

Traffic is slowing, congealing. Amazing how fast the pattern of the road changes. He moves into the middle lane. Slows a little. That'll annoy the lorry driver, but they're all going too fast. Teach them they can't rule the road. Size isn't everything.

... till Monday. Ok?

Yes, Monday's OK. She'll be more relaxed.

The lorry looms in the rear window.

Can't wait to ...

Grinning face.

Can't wait to what? See him?

Cars to both sides of him. And in front. There's nowhere to go.

Heart speeding.

Armpits sticky.

Every muscle rigid.

It's like a computer game.

But real.

Every car looks in control. But the tiniest swerve...

The smallest...

"I believe in Spinoza's God, who reveals Himself in the lawful harmony of the world, not in a God who concerns Himself with the fate and the doings of mankind."

Albert Einstein

"Anyone who is not shocked by quantum theory has not understood it."

– Niels Bohr
Danish physicist

"Shallow men believe in luck. Strong men believe in cause and effect."
Ralph Waldo Emerson

"Never expose yourself unnecessarily to danger; a miracle may not save you ... and if it does, it will be deducted from your share of luck or merit."
The Talmud

The Oedipus story: when King Laius and Queen Jocasta had baby boy, prophet Teiresias predicts he will kill father & marry mother. Laius tells servant to take baby far away & kill it. Servant can't face killing baby so leaves baby on hill. Baby rescued by shepherd & brought up by neighbouring king & queen. He doesn't know he's adopted. When baby grows up, learns of prophecy, but thinks adopted parents are real parents. Terrified in case prophecy comes true, he goes away. On journey he kills a man during an argument – surprise, surprise, it's King L, his real father. Arrives in city much later, goes to palace of Queen J, falls in love & marries her, not realizing it's his real mother. Moral of story: can't escape what fate has in store for you??????? Hate this story and all it stands for.

"We let go the present, which we have in our power, and look forward to that which depends upon chance, and so relinquish a certainty for an uncertainty."

Seneca

CHAPTER 30
TAILS

AN hour and a half later, Jess's father pulls up outside the hotel in central London and a valet parks the car while he walks into the hotel. He's already read the end of Jess's message. He hadn't really expected that she was going to say she couldn't wait to see him and sure enough she didn't.

Can't wait to leave school. It's all so weird now. Thinking of travelling with a friend and still maybe music college later but haven't sorted it yet. Let me know if Mon OK.

He'll email her back soon. But first, that glass of wine. He's tired and there's a definite headache brewing behind his eyes. So, a glass of wine, a hot shower and then a meal. And an early night.

There's nothing wrong with him that a decent sleep won't put right.

CHAPTER 31
TIME SLIDES

TIME has slipped by, speeding up. The prom is only a couple of days away. Jack and Jess spend almost all their hours together. Jess dares feel excited now about the future. It has more paths than barriers, more sunbeams than shadows.

Jack is teaching Jess to spin a coin. He says it's all in the mind, not the fingers. You *think* it into the air. You trace the path with your eyes and your heart. You send your soul with it. *It's easy*, he says, his eyes intent.

It's not as easy as he makes out, but Jess is happy enough for him to be so close to her, and laughing.

For laughing seems not to come so easily to him now. Not since, perhaps, the fairground. Or sometime around then. Time has blurred into a shapeless thing and it is hard to remember what happened on one day or another.

Jess needs Jack to carry on laughing. His face when she first saw it, around that music-room door, was wide and alive. Though how could she expect to know what dark currents ran beneath his surface? No one is only skin-deep. Although Jess senses that something is bothering him, she thinks it's just that the prom is only a couple of days away. Natural nerves – it's his band, after all, his passion. But Jess does not know that Jack is playing the game more and more now. From the moment he wakes till the time he goes to bed, he is snatching secret spins of the coin at every opportunity. He is hiding it from everyone: he senses that they would try to stop him, disapprove, laugh. But for Jack it is no laughing matter. It was never only a game for him, but now it's an addiction.

Jack is losing it. He is a boy who has clutched on to control ever since his second mother died, and he has needed to feel that good luck would follow him because of his actions, that nothing was chance, only a strange mix of fortune and reason, and now it's slipping away, the control, everything. Into somewhere very deep and very dark. He cannot explain why. All he knows is that what was once a deadly serious game is now just deadly serious.

Maybe it's something to do with facing the future, all this leaving school and childhood behind. He and Jess have talked about backpacking together in India, or somewhere, and that seems so exciting and yet so … huge, unanchored, full of too many possibilities. Or maybe love has simply knocked him upside down. And the more he understands how he so nearly didn't meet Jess, the more the idea terrifies him; the idea of all those infinite worlds of unknown possibilities has made him dizzy. He is falling into space.

Space is not far above us but everything is different there. There is no wind to carry you along and no one can hear you scream.

And so Jack continues to spin his coin and the people close to him notice only that he's perhaps a little thinner; there's darkness beneath his eyes; and his movements sometimes are jerky.

But still he laughs enough with Jess and touches her and loves her, so she will ignore the shadows and the sudden tiny absences, the times when she sees him staring into nothingness and his fingers become stone-still. We see what we want to see and Jess prefers not to see Jack falling into space.

She is ignoring her friends too. They have mostly returned from the courses or trips they've been on; and finished their exams, all of them now. She's had texts and emails and phone calls, which she's answered briefly. Yes, she's told Chloe and Farah that she's going out with Jack, and they will have told others, and yes, she's told them something about him, but we're talking the odd sentence or two and then *Gotta go – band practice!* Her friends are all talking about what to wear at the prom, but obviously Jess won't be wearing that sort of dress, though she's planned her outfit too. In fact, she bumped into Chloe and some of the others in the shopping mall, and they hugged and chatted and laughed but she felt strange. They messed around, joked about *lurve* and asked her to *Tell us everything and we mean everything*. But Jess found that as she started to tell them what Jack was like she couldn't properly explain him or what she felt. She'd always thought she'd want to tell her friends everything but now ... well, where do you start and how do you find the words? So she looked at her watch and pretended she was late.

She's had a bit of an email conversation with her dad too – and Monday is all sorted. She won't tell her mum this, but she's even, oddly, looking forward to seeing him. Especially as he seems to be encouraging the backpacking/ India/music-college idea. She hadn't planned to tell him so much so soon but there was a late night when she was fired up after band practice and couldn't sleep, so she'd gone online, found an email from him and replied; and he'd been online at the same time, so the reply came straight away, and it had kind of gone from there. In the darkness of her room, she had felt briefly disloyal to her mum, but she'd pushed that aside. She was doing nothing wrong.

Jess is beginning to believe that the future could hold all that she wants – Jack, music, everything. The strings that tie her down are loosening.

Sylvia, frankly, is falling to pieces. She was never particularly together in the first place, of course, but now she is quickly crumbling. Control is slipping from her like autumn leaves. Her husband is coming, no doubt insinuating his way between her and her daughter; he will unfold himself coolly from some sleek car and his eyes will trail over her body as though he is wondering what he ever saw in her; he will be wearing an expensive shirt and chinos, and shoes in soft brown leather; and she will look into his chocolate eyes and see Jessica and the past.

Added to that, her only daughter is going out with a boy who is stealing her heart and time. Her daughter is leaving school soon, which, as Sylvia knows – but is trying to forget – may change everything. No, let's face it, *will* change everything. Jess has occasionally used the words *gap year* and *travelling* in the past and Sylvia has had a clutching feeling in her throat every time. Even *India* and *backpacking* were mentioned the other day and Sylvia has a horrible intuition that a boyfriend may well make those words more likely to come true. They are such faraway words but yet they feel very close.

And Sylvia needs a drink. This needing a drink is odd – it's not like hunger or thirst, but a nagging in her mind, a pulling and tugging of her body towards wherever the drink is. It's like being a puppet on strings. Anyway, she'd found herself buying a bottle of gin from the supermarket, at the same time as picking up some of Jess's favourite foods – she plans to surprise Jess with a nice meal when she gets back from the boyfriend's house.

Sylvia's hands are shaking as she fumbles for her key. While she is opening the door, she doesn't even notice the haze of sweet peas and roses that tumble around the frame. There was a time, and not long ago either, when she couldn't walk past flowers without wanting to bury her face in the drowning scent of whatever was in bloom. Now, she just wants...

In the hall, Sylvia takes the bottle from her bag.

She looks at it. There is an ugly need in her. It has crept up on her, this need, over many months and maybe years, slowly and invisibly, and she does not exactly know when it turned from desire to need. It has played "grandmother's footsteps" with her mind. She wishes she could pour the contents of it down the sink but her fingers and feet will not allow her to do it. She knows that. It's the knowing that's the ugly bit. The drinking is the beautiful bit. How it floods over her like a warm wave and she can let herself sink into it and she forgets that anything matters.

The answering machine winks at her. She presses the button as she kicks her shoes off. It's Jess. Love snatches at her heart as she hears the voice. "Hi, Mum. Sorry but I won't be back till later. I'm eating at Jack's and then we'll probably practise some more. See you maybe about ten. I'll text you when I'm on my way."

Sylvia lets out a small noise. *Ohhh!* And suddenly fear and loneliness threaten to engulf her and stop her breathing. For a moment she thinks she could just sit there on the stairs and cry. But she does not. She stumbles towards the kitchen and opens the bottle. A quick swig settles her.

Jess, meanwhile, in Jack's bedroom, has just managed a very impressive spin of the coin. She plucks it from the air as it falls, closes her fingers over it and slaps it down on the back of her hand. Triumphantly.

"Heads or tails?" she asks.

"You haven't asked it a question."

"Yes, but heads or tails anyway?"

"But there's no point without a question."

"It's just a game though – a guessing game. It doesn't make any difference to anything."

"You're not taking it seriously." He frowns, not looking at her.

"Maybe you're taking it too seriously. You can't let it rule your life. God, Jack, we might as well believe in Farantella the Fantastic Fortune-teller! It's that stupid!"

He looks at her now. Seems about to say something. Takes her hands, slipping the coin from between them. He holds it in one hand, her hand in the other. He holds it up between her face and his, so he can see both: it is as though he does not know whether to look at her or the coin.

"But it does rule our lives, don't you see? And isn't it so much simpler that way? People say life's a lottery. But you don't know what you can change unless you try." He waves his hand towards the wall with all those newspaper stories. He carries on. "Life is serious and if you don't take it seriously it can creep up on you and…"

He pauses, looks away. Something plays across the muscles of his face. He swallows. Grabs her hands again, both of them. "You have to stay with me, Jess."

She is startled. "What's the matter? You look really weird."

"Thanks." And he smiles. At last, he smiles. "I love you, and I don't want you to go."

"I'm not going," she says, and she's not. Certainly, at that moment, she has no intention of going anywhere. Few people can resist being wrapped in love when it's offered. All dangers become invisible.

There's a shout from downstairs: Jack's dad. "Come and lay the table in five minutes. OK?"

Jack calls back that they'll be down. And then turns to Jess. "I have to tell you about my mother, how she died. Actually, twice, but I mean the second time." And he does. It is shocking and it brings tears to Jess's eyes. She hears it in silence, wanting to hold his hands, but they are clenched and white and she does not. He says it all while looking at a space above her head and then he looks at her.

"And that's why. Because it so shouldn't have happened and so nearly didn't. And if I'd kicked the ball differently or not asked her to play or whatever, then... And all of life's like that, Jess. All of it. Everything could be different. If only we did something different. Small things change everything."

She doesn't know what to say. She shakes her head, because it seems so wrong somehow. But she cannot see why.

He is still talking. "I so nearly didn't meet you. And now ... now..."

"What?"

"Something really bad could be about to happen."

"Or something really good could be about to happen."

"But what if it doesn't?"

"Can't we just focus on the things we can control?" Jess asks.

"Exactly! That's why I toss the coin. I can choose to do it. I can't control the way it lands but I can control whether I'm in the game. But now I think … it's controlling me. I'm doing it all the time. More than you think." He bites his lip.

"So stop playing it, Jack! Just stop doing it! If it's screwing you up."

"But…" And he looks at the newspaper cuttings again. "What if I stop and something terrible happens?"

"This is stupid. We don't know what's round the corner and, if we did, what would we do about it? Like Oedipus in that story. Trying to escape the prophecy he ends up doing exactly what the prophecy said. He can't escape."

"Yeah, I know – had to do an essay on it in philosophy. It tangles me up – like, if he'd never been *told* he was going to kill his father and marry his mother, he'd never have done it, and yet it was only trying to avoid it that made it all come true. If he'd ignored it he'd have been fine. I hate that story. It's … I don't know … cruel. It gives us no power or choice at all. Just makes everything pointless. But that's not what I'm talking about – I'm not talking about knowing what's round the corner. I'm talking about the fact we have to decide which corner to walk round. That's what the coin does."

"Yes, *we* have to decide, not some coin. You're handing your life over to a *coin* – Christ, Jack! You have to stop this." And as she says it, she knows it is true.

Jack takes a deep breath, shifts his thoughts into gear.

Remember, Jack has equilibrium. Push him however far and he'll spring back. He's not the sort of person to go to pieces, though anyone can crack a little now and then. Besides, you can paper over cracks and sometimes that's enough. There is a moment, a seesaw point, where he may tip over, and then, "Better watch out for things beginning with 'w', hadn't we?" He grins. "Come on – we need to lay the table. But first, how about you take the coin? Then I can't use it any more. Keep it with you. Don't let me have it back."

"I think that sounds like a very good idea."

He spins it one last time, catches it behind his back, one-handed, without looking.

"Show-off!"

Jack hands her the coin. It is warm from his hand. She looks at it, puts it in her pocket. He flicks hair from his eyes. "OK? Let's go. After you."

She leaves the room before him and does not see him take one long look at the newspaper stories before he follows her.

A few minutes later, they are chatting over lasagne with Jack's father. Laughter and stories, stainless steel and granite that sparkles, warm lighting, steaming bread and shining faces. At some point, they get on to the subject of what they're going to do next. The backpacking to India thing comes up and Sam takes a deep breath before smiling. "God, I'm jealous of you two: your whole lives ahead of you. And you'd leave an old man like me to hobble towards my pension?"

More laughter.

They cannot know what is round the corner, or which corner they may soon walk round. Because at the moment there is nothing round the corner; there is not, yet, even any corner. Just possibilities.

CHAPTER 32
THE DAY BEFORE
THE PROM

THE night of the prom is approaching fast.

Jess brushes everything else into a corner of her mind – her mum, her friends, what to eat for breakfast. Even the idea that she is about to leave school does not seem real – it is as though she left ages ago and she is somewhere else already. She is another person, and her cells breathe differently. The future holds fewer fears now that she is not standing on the edge alone.

The band, the prom and Jack. When she sings with them there is nothing else to think about.

Jack does not mention the coin now, seems to have forgotten the game. He has not forgotten: he is just hiding it. But he is hiding it well. Perhaps, if he can avoid playing it for long enough, the patterns of his thoughts may change and the desire fade.

But he cannot help worrying. Ever since he can remember, he has beckoned good luck by sacrificing himself to fortune, thinking he can change invisible particles. Maybe he was right. What if by stopping now he will attract bad fortune? He tries – tries so hard – to block this worry out and to be reasonable.

The trouble is that Jack is finding it hard to shake off the fear that something bad may be about to happen. Jess has seemed able to dismiss the Farantella thing. And every sensible part of Jack has done the same. But... No, it is ridiculous. If he believed that stuff, he should be avoiding red, and boats (or planes or things with wings), and big things in the water, and things beginning with 'w'. Which would be plain silly. And with this thought he tries to drown the fear. *Ridiculous, ridiculous*, he repeats to himself when it tries to squeeze its way back in.

In Jack's garage, they bury themselves in songs. Each song has been sung many times, and mostly it has been about technique, dynamics, getting the words right, making sure each instrument blends perfectly with the others, or takes its turn in dominating. They have done a full run-through several times and each time it has been better. It has become somewhat routine-y for Jess. This is no bad thing, because then the emotion and nerves of the night will carry it to a new level. You wouldn't want to reach your peak in rehearsal.

But sometimes, even in practice, the music carries her away. She slides into the colours and lets the fingers of the notes touch her. And when this happens she looks up afterwards and sees Jack watching her and smiling and then nothing is bad in the world at all.

The night before the prom arrives.

They have an early evening practice and decide that they are as ready as they will ever be. "See you tomorrow," say Chris, Ella and Tommy as they leave Jack's house.

"Want to eat here?" Jack asks Jess.

"Are you sure that's OK with your dad? I seem to have been here a lot."

"No problem. He likes you – he's got good taste."

Her phone rings. It's her mum. "It's me – hope you're going to be back soon? I've cooked."

Jess makes a face at Jack as she answers. "You've cooked? Sounds like a good reason to steer clear." She doesn't feel like joking. Jack is signalling that it's OK, that she should go. And she knows he's right.

Her mum again: "Please, Jess. We'll have a nice evening. Your last as a schoolgirl." Jess rolls her eyes. A couple of weeks ago and she wouldn't have been so irritated by this emotional stuff. She shifts from foot to foot, trying to decide. Jack nods at her.

"OK, Mum. I'll be about half an hour."

"I thought you were at Jack's?"

"I am."

"You told me it took less than fifteen minutes to walk there."

"Well, I'm in the middle of something."

"Fine. Oh, can you get some single cream from the corner shop – just a small one? Oh, and a lemon. I forgot them."

Rolls her eyes again. "Is that all?"

"Maybe some chocolate. Something you like."

Jess finishes the conversation quickly and a little over half an hour later, she is home. Jack has not come with her this time – he's got things to do for tomorrow.

Spike rolls on the path in front of her, catching the last bit of sun before it disappears beneath the trees. Jess stops to tickle his tummy and she loves how he stretches. Lucky Spike – so little to worry about.

Sylvia is in the kitchen in some degree of happy chaos. She is drinking a glass of wine as she cooks, and humming to herself. "Hello, Jessie darling! Oh, thanks – did you get everything I needed?" And she twitters on about what she's cooking, not leaving any space for Jess to speak.

There is a lit candle wafting lily scent into the air and the kitchen table is nicely laid. Sylvia pours Jess a glass of wine. "Sit down, Jessie. I'm doing everything tonight." But Jess can't sit down for long because suddenly the sauce is ready at the same time as the rice and there's no salad dressing because Sylvia's forgotten to make it. Jess deals with the rice and the dressing. Sylvia is flapping. She's not drunk, but her brain is not entirely engaged.

Soon, they are eating.

"It's great, Mum." And it is, surprisingly: chicken strips in a creamy lemon sauce, and wild rice with splashes of fresh coriander leaf. The salad is casual but has all the right things in it and is herby from their own garden.

"So, tell me all about tomorrow. What happens

and what are you wearing? And everything. Are you nervous? I wish I could see you – do you think…?"

"No, Mum, you can't! But maybe one day, hey? Come and see us play somewhere." And they chat on about just this and that but really nothing is *just* this and that any more, because anything can open up the earthquake crack. Anything they might talk about is likely to be the future, and that is a frightening place for Sylvia.

Sylvia should not say what she is about to say. But she has had at least two drinks now and that is the risk. She really does not want to bring up the subject, *really* does not want to. But she does.

"Are you still thinking of backpacking in India?" Her fork picks a leaf out of the rice. The other hand twiddles the stem of her near-empty glass.

"I expect so. We haven't had much time to think about it yet."

"Well, don't you need a plan? Like, you can't just *go*, can you? And what about the money? And is Jack definitely to be trusted?"

Now there's a good question.

"Look, Mum, you have to trust me. And of *course* Jack… What are you suggesting?"

"Nothing, just that you haven't known him long."

"Oh God, that old one. We're together, Mum, seriously, and we want to go together. We've not planned any details yet though – let's just wait till after tomorrow, hey?"

"And the money?"

Why is it that jaw muscles clench? "I can get a job – in a shop or anything. And anyway, we're going to busk. Jack's serious about the band. So am I." Sylvia may be arty and floaty and dippy but she's also a mother and it's the mother part that shrinks at the idea of her daughter and boyfriend in a band. Which is why she can't say, *How lovely for you, darling*.

"How long will you go for?" Sylvia pours herself another glass. The wine splashes. With her finger, she wipes up some spillage.

"Don't know. A few months. And I'm definitely going to apply to music college for next year."

"That's expensive though. You mean the local one?"

"No, Mum, proper music college. London."

Sylvia flinches. How could she not have known? Of course, she did know – not that it would be London but that it would not be here – but she has been shutting it out.

The glass is half empty. Silence sinks over them. Spike, on the windowsill, opens one eye.

"But, Jess, that's going to be *so* expensive." Of course, she's right, but that's not what she's most worried about. She's just thinking that her little girl in London is such a scary thought. London is so big and Jess is so ... so needed here.

A pause. "Dad's going to pay, I think." Of course he is.

"When did he say that? The bastard! How does he

think that makes me feel?" Red spots have formed on Sylvia's cheeks and there's a sheen on her forehead.

"Mum, it's not about *you*! Dad can afford it and it's what I really want. You both always said I should use my musical talent – well, now I am. And this is not a new idea. And, God, Mum, kids leave home, you know. You don't want me to be one of those sad people who live with their parents until they're old themselves, do you?"

"Well…"

"Well, that's stupid."

There is a silence that seems longer than it is, and Sylvia twiddles the stem of her glass, her lips twitching, but no words coming out. "No, of course I don't. I'm only joking. Now, how about some ice cream? I got mint choc chip," she says, her eyes bright.

Jess stopped liking mint choc chip about five years ago but she does not remind Sylvia. They eat it together and Sylvia does not drink any more wine. Or at least not while Jess is there. And when, a little later, Jess says she's going upstairs to get her outfit ready and have a bath and an early night, Sylvia behaves perfectly, even though she'd have loved to sit up longer with her daughter on such a night. Jess doesn't notice this perfect behaviour; she is not thinking about her mother now. Sylvia is like the little girl who has such a reputation for naughtiness that no one notices the one time she is not bad.

Someone should give Sylvia credit for her effort that

night. It may mark the beginning of her improvement, or this may be too much to hope for.

As darkness settles on Jack and Jess and the people connected to them, many possibilities shift into position. All the particles and laws of motion, all the immeasurable and unpredictable forces roll on. That's the science of it. But instead, we merely ask, *Who will be lucky and who will not?*

What Jack might ask is: *Is there anything that I should do differently?*

Differently from what?

Differently from whatever it is I'm going to do.

But what are you going to do?

I don't know, but whatever it is.

If you're going to do it, you're going to do it.

But I could do it differently, if I knew.

Then you wouldn't be going to do it.

For nothing is decided. The Oedipus story is an exercise in thought, a nonsense story not of the real world. And the only way to deal with it is not to believe it. Same with Farantella the Fortune-teller: if you believe her, you are doomed. If things turn out to fit with her prediction, it will only be a coincidence.

CHAPTER 33
SYLVIA TRIES

SYLVIA has bought Jess flowers for this day. And she has another gift: a beautiful framed picture of tall Californian poppies dancing strong in the wind, which Sylvia has painted herself. She has written a note and put it with the presents, leaving them outside Jess's door before she wakes up. This has involved hiding the flowers the night before, which is a feat of forward-planning most unlike Sylvia. It has also involved Sylvia not being hung over, so that she can get up before her daughter. So, no, she did not drink any more after we left her last night. Which is nothing short of a miracle but just shows what is possible.

The note says, *Thinking of you today, Jess! Hope you have a wonderful evening. All my love always, Mum xxxx.*

Jess, when she comes down to the kitchen later and finds her mother drinking coffee and eating toast, just like anyone, gives Sylvia a hug and a smile and a breezy

Thank you, Mum. That was so sweet. She looks round and sees no detritus from the night before, feels the fresh air through the open window, smells bacon ready for a roll with her favourite mustard and ketchup.

She sees no fragile look in her mother's eyes, because she does not look for it, does not want to find it. She feels only happiness and excitement for herself. It is all she wants to feel this particular day. The last day of the first part of her life.

Sylvia is trying. She really is. It is not a daughter's job to spot fragile looks in a mother's eyes.

CHAPTER 34
JESS'S DAD

JESS'S dad, Lorenzo, is not thinking about Jess. He has work to do and he is one of those people who can shut things away until they are needed. He has already sent her a present, which the woman in the shop had assured him that his daughter – even though she has never met her – would like. It is a silver bracelet of intricate and unusual design. He has sent her some money too, to buy herself something special to mark this important day.

And he has ordered flowers and a bottle of champagne to be delivered during the day. Isn't that the sort of thing you do when your daughter leaves school? He is not entirely sure but he does it anyway. Then, once the credit card has gone through, he puts it all from his mind and focuses on his paper on genetics.

He loves genetics: so beautifully mathematical. It follows rules, and once you know the rules and the behaviour of the particles then you can begin to make wonderfully accurate predictions.

Lorenzo is not someone who concerns himself with thoughts of luck. He looks for more scientific answers. If this, then that; if that, then this follows. It makes him smile.

CHAPTER 35
A LADDER

JACK and Jess are about to walk underneath a ladder.

It's Jack's fault. More or less. They would have walked past but he'd stopped.

"Why don't we walk underneath it? Are you afraid?"

"Dangerous things, ladders," Jess says, pretending to look serious. "A pot of paint could fall on you as you walk under it."

"There's no paint there. It's just a ladder. No one's even on it."

"I don't know. It makes more sense to walk around it though. Even apart from the fact that it's supposed to be unlucky."

"Yeah, but that's rubbish, isn't it? It's supposed to be unlucky to walk on the cracks in the pavement too, but I don't see you taking notice of that."

"Yeah, but ladders — I don't know, it would feel weird to walk under it."

"Toss you for it?"

"I thought you weren't playing that game any more."

"I'm not. You've got the coin, remember. If you don't want to, we don't have to. It's totally your choice."

Is there an extra intensity in Jack's eyes? Is there anything to watch out for here? Or is it just any old moment, not a moment that matters?

"I say we don't use the coin," says Jess. "We just *decide* ourselves, without the coin. Free will."

"Excellent! So, how do we decide? Let's say you have free will: which way will you go? I'll follow you." He wheels around to face her.

She laughs. Closes her eyes. Looks inside her head. Under the ladder? Not under the ladder? Follow superstition? Or not? Use science? Or emotion?

It's not easy, this. Deciding this way or that when there's no real reason to choose one more than the other. Avoid the ladder, because that's normal? Or go under it because it's interesting? Avoid it because superstition might be right? Go under it because *of course* superstition is ancient rubbish?

Decide, Jess. It doesn't matter.

Or does it?

Of course it's easy. All you have to do is choose.

A red car flashes past, its silencer broken so that it explodes its noise into the air. It makes her jump, kind of grates on her feelings.

She decides. She thinks.

Grabs Jack's hand and pulls him after her.

They slide beneath the ladder together and run down the pavement, laughing.

CHAPTER 36
THE KELLY GANG

KELLY and her friends are being preened and coiffed and made-up at Samantha's house. They've had a glass or two of cheap fizzy wine already. After all, they won't be allowed much at the prom, not with the teachers there to keep an eye on things.

Doesn't matter though. Kelly and her friends have other plans. The main part of the plan involves vodka. And a desire to disrupt Schrödinger's Cats in some way – to do something to take the arrogant smirks off the faces of Jack and Jess. Everything else is unplanned: they'll go with the flow. After the prom they're lined up to go to Simon's house. His dad own a speedboat and jet skis. He's stinking rich.

They're not bad girls, not really. It's just that they don't think very much. They're just girls who want to have fun.

Should be an amazing party.

CHAPTER 37
JACK'S DAD

JACK'S dad, Sam, has driven the band to the school in his van. After unloading everything and helping them set up, he gets ready to leave. He plans to come back in the morning to collect it all again, with Jack and the others to help, once they can get themselves out of bed. The things parents do for their kids.

"Break a leg and all that!" And he smiles at his son, and at Jess. They thank him. "You look great," he tells her. And she does. A short green and black dress with lots of netting in the skirt part, tight corset thing on top. Leggings underneath. Little shoes, which she's going to kick off once she's on stage. Her hair is a waterfall of black ice. Her eyes shine.

Jack and Jess hurry away, forgetting him as he stands there watching. He lingers, just looking, thinking. He is pleased for Jack, glad that he has met Jess. She seems like a lovely girl.

Lucky boy. And he deserves it. Hope it works out. That he's happy.

And then – of course: *If only Liz could have been here.* There is always that thought, lurking, ready to swoop out. But he's pretty good at shutting it back in again. And it's a weird thought, because it's not Liz, but his first wife, Jane, who should really be there.

He turns away then. Job done. And he drives back home. He'll watch a DVD, maybe do a bit of work. He can't imagine getting much sleep, not tonight. There's too much in the air. He should have organized to go out with some friends. Tessa wasn't free that evening because she had some family thing to go to involving her own younger kids. Tessa is someone you might call his girlfriend, though it is more casual and yet more important than that. Tessa would understand how he feels this night, but he also would not have wanted to take her from her own kids. Jack's dad is too nice for bad stuff to happen to him; though, as we know, that hasn't helped him in the past.

It's funny how it gets to you. Special days. Although this is Jess's prom, it marks the end of Jack's schooldays too. And how can he think of this without thinking of that awful first day?

But he must not think about it too much. It screws you up if you let your mind dwell too much on pain, he knows. And so he enters the house and flings a few prawns and spices together to make his favourite curry. Pours a glass of wine and sits down to see if there's anything worth watching on TV. If not, it'll be a DVD. It won't make much difference one way or the other: it's going to be a long evening.

But the forecast for tomorrow is perfect for surfing, so he looks forward to that.

CHAPTER 38
SYLVIA FAILS

SYLVIA is drunk. She wasn't planning to be, but she is remembering Jess's face as she opened the bracelet and money from her father, after breakfast that morning. And then the flowers and champagne had arrived, bigger and more expensive flowers than Sylvia's. Of course, Jess is allowed to be happy. Sylvia knows her reaction is irrational. But that's the whole point about being Sylvia.

Now she is staring at the bottom of an empty glass, wondering who emptied it. And if we stay and watch for too long, we may see a tear fall, and we will be torn between pity and irritation.

CHAPTER 39
SPIKE

SPIKE jumps in through the catflap. He has been hunting hot summer mice in the night. But suddenly he feels a need to be home. Softly, he slips through the kitchen and up the stairs, straight into Jess's room.

It is very empty. He sniffs the air. He does not like it. Something. What it is he does not know but his back feels all itchy. A shiver runs along it. His hairs stand on end. The tip of his tail flicks from side to side.

He pads to the window, leaps onto the windowsill, weaving between the photos and fat candles, and looks out. The night is thick and warm but not quite dark. It won't be. It's that time of year. Good for hunting.

Spike jumps down and then onto Jess's bed, where he pummels the duvet before he curls himself round and round and round into the smell of her. Still unrelaxed, he begins to wash. It is comforting and rhythmical. But it is not enough.

Eventually, Spike falls into a troubled sleep, and in that sleep his whiskers twitch. There is a pricking of his hackles. He dreams, and in those dreams something nasty this way comes.

CHAPTER 40
LOST IN MUSIC

JESS is losing her place in space. Every part of her is unravelling in the lights, the dancing shadows, the music that is so loud that it rocks her cells. It is hard not to scream with pure, raw joy. Her heart is so full that it hurts. This is power. It is better than anything.

She sings in bare feet. It feels more real, gives her more balance. Her black leggings make her legs look even longer than they are. Her hair is beginning to straggle, sweaty tendrils hanging over her eyes and sticking to her cheeks. There is the feel of it on her bare shoulders.

She knows they are playing better than ever in rehearsal. It's obvious from the dancers, the whooping at the end of each song, as the music crashes and hurls itself at them, or fades into a soft fractional silence. There is Jack, his swooping hair wild, just as she loves it, the streaks glinting in the spotlights, his eyes bright, shoulders crouched over the instrument as his long thin guitarist's fingers find each chord. The volume shakes her bones: it is physical.

So hard do they concentrate that it is easy to forget, mostly, that among the dancers are Kelly, Samantha and Charlie, stringing along whichever boys they are playing with that night. Simon may be there, though he does not go to Northseas High. But none of that matters, not to Jess and Jack, who are wrapped up in music. For Chris, Ella and Tommy, as well, the Kelly thing is not worth thinking about. This is not her night. This is the night for Schrödinger's Cats.

Between two songs, while Jack and Chris make adjustments to their guitars, Jess takes a couple of mouthfuls of water; she looks out over the audience, blinking against the spotlights. People are watching her and she loves that feel of their eyes. Among them are Chloe and Farah, with Paul and Marco; and there's Abby and Christa and Toni and … is that Dan with blue hair? They wave at her and shout, and she grins back, doing a thumbs-up. Farah makes gestures towards Jack, a face of approval, and Jess catches Jack's look, grins again. Her heart tumbles and if she could see her own eyes she would see the pupils widen.

The night spins along. Faster. And no one is predicting anything. They are happy in the moment and are looking no further.

Soon it is time for her song. Jess moves to the front of the stage, where someone has put her stool. The floor is dusty beneath her feet. She barely hears Jack introducing her, just senses the settling of the audience. The wolf-whistles. Her heart begins to race – she can hear it in her head. She must steady it. Deep breaths. Sip of water. Take your time.

There's a crash at the back of the hall. Broken glass. A murmur from the floor, people turning. Kelly's head is thrown back and laughing. She stumbles. Shouts something, nothing. Two teachers move towards the commotion and there is some kind of argument. Jess puts it aside and focuses on what she is there for. Those losers can't touch her. They are not part of this, nor of any part of her life. She will shut them out of everything.

Jess takes the guitar and adjusts the strap around her neck. Looks at Jack. A bubble of breath ticks in her throat. He is sitting a little way from her, holding the sand-shaker, ready when she is, ready to keep to her beat. His shirt sticks to his body with sweat; his thin tie is loosened around his throat. Jess perches on the stool, one bare foot on a crossbar, the other on the floor. Uses her toes to balance perfectly. She feels the hard wood under her skin.

Tommy is gently skiffling the drums, his black hair sweaty on his forehead; Ella is fingering the keyboard and rippling clever rhythms while they wait.

They are all ready. Silence. Jess makes eye contact with each of them, a small nod. *Two – three – four* and into the shifting hush she strums the first chord and begins to sing. "The Colour of Loss". And the band plays around her, softly, so that her voice is swept over them.

Noise at the back of the hall. *Ignore it. Kelly will not spoil this.*

As she flows into her song, squeezes out the emotion of the words, blends the tones, this time, at last, she *is* thinking about the meaning while she sings. She wonders, *Is grief ever beautiful? Or is it, in fact, always dark?* This time it wrings her out, marbles her with a sadness she has never experienced but can now imagine all too well. It's not just a song any more.

> "I didn't mean to lose you,
> I'd have done it on a different day,
> If I had known
> If I had known another way
> I'd have breathed a longer breath
> Walked a twisted path
> Danced a slower beat
> Laughed a softer laugh
> If I had known
> We had no other day.
> And then again I'd say
> I only need a sadder song
> And you'd be gone.
> For there is no other way."

And as she finishes that chorus one last time and the noise of the crowd swells, she looks at Jack and she can tell that she has touched something in him. Perhaps because of the emotion of the night, perhaps because she understands now about his mother. Who knows, but certainly this is a moment where there is more meaning than can be spoken.

"If I had known…" But what she realizes in that moment is that you can't. To imagine knowing the future is like imagining waking up in the morning and you're a cockroach: not worth thinking about because it wouldn't be this world, and you wouldn't be you. You'd be a cockroach in another world.

Pretty pointless. Unlike this world, the real one, the only one, the one in which you have to make choices.

CHAPTER 41
STRANGE HOT TEARS

STRANGE hot tears and the smell of Jack as Jess buries her face in his neck. Feeling faint. She lifts her mouth to his. His hand on her back, crushing her to him. His lips on hers, his tongue. Fingers beneath her chin, holding her up. She is pressed against a wall as a warm night wind blows around them, chilling the sweat on her arms. Jess shivers.

"You are brilliant. Beautiful." He wipes a tear from her cheek. "And silly."

Ella is calling them. "Are you two coming or not?"

They disentangle themselves, more or less, and walk together towards where Ella is waiting with Chris, Tommy and some others. Jess has already said goodbye to some of her friends – they're going to a club and maybe a party in someone's house. Jack and Jess are off to the beach with a different crowd. Bonfire, some chips from the chippy on their way, a few drinks, watch the stars, toast marshmallows. They've even brought the marshmallows with them – "Hanging on to our childhoods a bit longer," Ella had said. An after-show beach party was the plan. And on such a warm night, with a soft Saharan wind, Jess can think of nothing better. She wants fresh air, not the staleness of a hundred other people. Yes, she'd have liked her other friends to come too but nothing matters more than being with Jack, and she will see them again often anyway. It is not goodbye. But she wants to keep hold of every moment of this night.

She has the coin in her back pocket, because Jack made sure she had it with her before she left her house all those hours ago.

"Just in case."

"Just in case what?"

"Just in case we *decide* to use it, of course." And he grinned at her, his hair swooping over one eye. He'd done a complicated job with the styling gel for this evening. Now, of course, his hair is all over the place. Well, it is always all over place, but now this is chaotically so, rather than designed.

And now, at one in the morning and the sky ebony clear, eating fat chips from paper steamy with vinegar, he is not thinking about the coin. He is not thinking about the game which has ruled the last few years of his life. Or the stories of people like Tommy Allsup and the guy who'd been killed by a tortoise falling on his head. It is an exaggeration to say he has forgotten – rather, he has put it away in a cupboard and closed the door. It may be lurking but it is hidden. And the Farantella thing is concealed in shadows. Even Jack's done a pretty good job of dismissing her warning as nonsense. Logic appears to be winning.

A growing wind gusts around them, bringing a dry unexpected heat. There is the smell of seaweed and salt. The bars along the front fade far into the background as they all walk further along the beach, to the end, almost by the rocks.

The surf is strong tonight, smashing against the shore. Moonlight shines on the white froth as it stretches far out, curling and fuming.

Loudly they walk, all of them, along the sea wall away from the town. Though "walk" is quite the wrong word for what they do. They balance, teeter, joke around. They bowl along, like leaves skittering in a breeze.

Behind them, the noise and lights become tiny. Everyone jumps down onto the beach, some of them stumbling, others deliberately falling, kicking the sand with their toes. Ella runs towards the water's edge and Chris runs after her. They splash through the shallows. Jess has a sweatshirt and jeans on now and she has kicked off her shoes again. She is neither too hot nor too cold. Everything feels right. There are no shadows for Jess tonight. She has thoughts for no place but here, no time but now.

"Let's get the fire going," says Tommy. And they look around for driftwood in the tidemarks and further away from the wall, in the stubby grasses where the beach ends. Soon, a sizeable pile has grown and Tommy has taken over the construction.

They are prepared with matches for the fire and a couple of rugs and plastic glasses and some bottles of cheap drink. Thought has gone into this evening. There are several small groups, who begin make their own fires along the beach. Tonight, the beach belongs to them, as the fluid friendships of recent years gather and separate like oil on water.

Soon Jack and Jess's group are sitting or lying around the crackling fire. Wood snaps and sparks. Wind tears the flames, ripping at them, wafting sharp smoke away. Jack has his arm around Jess and she leans against him. They are looking towards the sea, drinks in hands.

Jess is drinking vodka. Not much. And slowly. She has no desire to miss any moment of this night. Jack, too. Getting drunk is not part of their plan. He stretches for the bottle of lemonade and they top up their drinks with that. Some are drinking more, but everyone is in control. They talk and laugh and everything is more than usual: the sky is bigger, the stars more numerous, the crashing of the waves louder. And the flames surge higher as Tommy brings more and more wood. He is the King of the Wood-gatherers, he has decided.

Marshmallows are speared on to sticks and held over the flames. Sugar shrivels and drops and hisses. The tips of tongues test the burnt caramel. Soft squelching in the mouth, creamy fullness and a sweet taste. Melting marshmallow is great dipped in vodka, they discover.

The fire toasts their faces. Jack wipes a smoky smudge from Jess's nose.

"Let's play a game," says Chris.

"Spin the bottle?" suggests Ella.

"Good idea," calls someone from a nearby group, joining them.

"Need to finish it first." And Tommy does. He tries spinning it but finds that you can't spin a bottle properly on a sandy beach. A frown corrugates his forehead as he struggles to change the laws of nature.

"Or something with dares."

"Like what?"

"Tossing a coin," says Ella. "You call and if you're wrong everyone else gets to choose a dare."

Jack looks at Jess. She shrugs. It sounds like harmless fun. It could be. If we look back on it afterwards, we will not call it harmless fun, but that doesn't help us now.

If we look for meaning, we find meaning where perhaps no meaning really is. There could be no meaning at all. It could just be life. Stuff happening, doing your best.

"Your turn first, Ella. It was your idea." Chris takes a coin from his wallet inside his jacket pocket. Ella grins and runs a hand through her spiked hair till it looks even more like a straw nest. Her thick black eyeliner is all smudged with sweat and probably the tears of so many goodbyes. She has an elfin face, thinks Jess.

Ella calls heads. It's tails. "Unlucky!" they all shout.

Jess leans back into Jack's body, feels his arms tight around her and his mouth in her hair. Her hands are on his and she is learning the geography of his knuckles.

"Pour her a drink," says someone.

"No, I'm not doing that," says Ella. "That's a stupid dare."

"Play the game, Ella," says Tommy. Tommy is drunk, not badly so but enough to say things he wouldn't normally say. He's in the mood not to care, not to think before he speaks.

"Give me something else to do."

"Oh, come on, what's the point of a dare if you don't do it?"

Ella looks angry. She shakes her head. Something nasty descends on the group. Into their silence the fire cracks more loudly and the wild surf roars like a beast.

Jess butts in. "Just give her something else. She doesn't have to play drinking games. How about a blindfold obstacle course?"

The moment is broken as they set about creating an obstacle course for Ella to negotiate blindfold.

"Hey, you're sending me to the sea!" Ella shouts as she feels her feet going down the sloping beach. But she laughs as the first wave crashes over her feet, soaking her jeans to the knees.

"Go and rescue her, Chris!" Jack laughs. And Chris runs down the beach, scooping up Ella and carrying her back still blindfolded. As she watches them, Jess sees a light out at sea, and a shape. Two lights. Speedboats?

"Jet skis," says Jack, seeing where she is looking.

"Bit stupid to do that at night, isn't it?"

"Dunno. Some idiots, that's all."

And they turn back to the game. It is Jack's turn and he extricates himself from Jess in order to arm-wrestle Tommy – Jack wins and Tommy has to drink another shot. And so the game continues with forfeits which only seem funny at the time – bum prints in the sand, vodka drunk from someone else's belly button, a marshmallow eaten from someone's lips, running semi-naked to the next fire and stealing an item, passing a hand through the flames, twenty press-ups, singing "Baa, Baa, Black Sheep" while standing on your head.

The jet skis skim and leap over the bay again, closer now. They can hear shrieking across the waves, see the lights skittering here and there. The unnatural drone is annoying. It is not much louder than the surf and the fires and the laughter of friends, but it is intrusive.

"Isn't that Kelly?" says Ella, after a while, when one jet ski has roared towards the beach and then turned and disappeared again.

She is right. That blonde hair stands out in the moonlight and, as the light from the other jet ski shines briefly on her body, they can see she's wearing a bright red top of some sort now, maybe a life jacket, though it doesn't quite look like one. If Jess looked round at Jack now, she'd see him frown.

They turn away, not wishing to let Kelly spoil their party, reckoning that if they ignore her she'll soon go.

The marshmallows have finished but someone has crisps. Tommy has fallen asleep and has to be prodded awake when it's his turn. A couple of the other groups have dispersed now, the flames of their fires sinking into embers. Ash blows in the wind. The smell of burning wood is in Jess's hair, her eyes, her skin. And Jack's. She can smell him through it as she leans back against him. She pulls his arms more tightly around her as she sits between his legs. Jack has drunk very little, Jess little more: she is gently floating, her skin tingling in a pleasant woolly way.

Energy is seeping away from the night but they want to cling to it. Despite the quickening wind, the growing waves, it is still warm. The tide is coming in, the surf hurling itself hungrily at the beach. But their group is far from the water's edge, on sand that is always dry.

Jess has pins and needles. She extricates herself from Jack and stands up, moving her feet and toes to get the blood flowing again.

It is Jack's turn.

"Oh, let's stop now," says Ella. "I've had enough. Sand in places that are going to be hard to explain."

But Tommy and Chris have other ideas. "Everyone else has done two," says Tommy.

"Yeah, well, you're seeing two of everything, Tommy," says Jack.

But of course, Jack will do it. One last turn. And then they'll stop, they agree.

"Let me spin the coin," says Jess. They wait for her.

She holds out her hand for someone to give her the coin. "Well, who's got it?"

"Tommy, you had it last."

"Well, I haven't got it now." Tommy vaguely looks around him. They all search but no one can find it.

"Just use another one," says Ella.

Jess takes the one from her back pocket. Jack's coin. The one she's been keeping safe. Maybe if she hadn't been drinking, she'd have kept it safe still.

"Jack?"

He hesitates.

"What's the big deal?" asks Chris. He looks from Jack to Jess. Their faces look oddly serious. Intent.

Still Jack hesitates. It is as though the words will not come from his mouth. In his head he is stuck; his brain will not send the instruction to the mouth. *Yes?* Or *No?* It's simple and yet, as he very well knows, not so simple. Because it may well make a difference, and he will never know.

"It won't make any difference which coin you use," says someone.

"You have no idea if it will or won't."

"It's just a coin, Jack, for Christ's sake. It's just a coin. Like, *game*, you know? As in *game*?" Tommy has a headache. He has no time for his friend's pointless hang-ups. He has known Jack for a long time, has seen him obsess about this damned coin – not that Tommy knows that this is not the original coin. But if he did, it would make no difference: a coin is a coin and simply the best way we have to imitate randomness. Chance. Luck. Tommy doesn't care what you call it. Tommy is like most people.

Jack stares at Tommy for what seems a long time. Jess kneels down, touches his arm. "Hey, Jack, don't spoil things. I don't mind what coin we use. Maybe let's not even play, hey? It's late. Maybe we should go home soon? I'm getting a bit cold anyway."

And after a moment Jack relaxes. Shrugs. "It's OK. Let's do it. As you say, Tommy, it won't make any difference, will it?" And he pours himself a small shot of vodka, knocking it back. "Go for it, Jess. Spin that coin. And make it a good spin."

He puts his hand on hers to slant her fingers the right way, watches as she balances the coin in just the place where he has taught her. And she spins.

It is a good spin. It is beautiful. The firelight catches it, the wind catches it, Jack blows a kiss towards her and the kiss catches it. The coin flies high, hovers, tumbles down, and Jack calls heads.

It is tails. He stands up, runs his hands through his hair. "So, what's it to be?"

"Skinny-dipping," says someone.

"Easy," says Jack. "I could do with washing all this smoke off me." He kicks off his shoes. There is wolf-whistling as he strips off: rugby shirt, T-shirt, trainers, socks, jeans. Chris puts his hands over Jess's eyes. There is laughter again. The wind catches the flames and they stretch and lean. Jess hugs her knees.

There are the jet skis, far away in the distance. Light plays over the water like two tiny Tinkerbells. Everyone watches and laughs as Jack runs towards the water, splashes through the first shallow frothy breakers, and dives forward smooth as a porpoise.

There is a moment of emptiness. It is a fraction of space, when one thing ends and another begins. Laughter stops, punched in the face, shocked.

Jess's body freezes.

Breath holds.

One jet ski.

It is coming.

Straight

towards

the beach.

Jack is standing now,

his back to the sea,

grinning.

The rider's face

laughing,

but then

terrified,

trying to turn.

Screaming.

A spray of froth.

A flash

of red.

Jack.

CHAPTER 42
SPLINTERS OF TIME

TIME moves backwards. Splinters. It is impossible to say what happens first. The jet ski almost misses Jack. It catches him a glancing blow and his rag-doll body is flung through the air, before landing in the shallows.

Jess cannot scream. Or breathe.

A body flies from the jet ski. The jet ski hits the body in the air before skimming onto the beach.

Jack swallows bitter water.

Blood.

The coin digs into Jess's hand, bruising it.

People run towards the water's edge.

Someone dials 999. Three others do the same. They cannot see the buttons. Fingers are all thick and useless. They shake.

Jess is at the water's edge ahead of them. Her mind is full of one word only:

No!

CHAPTER 43
SCREAMING

IF...

If Jack had not met Jess, she would be somewhere else entirely. She would be nowhere near this beach with its faraway town lights, running screaming along the shingle towards the human heap that sprawls in the froth, her clothes sticky with sweat and sea spray and vodka and grimy with wood smoke.

Jack wouldn't be here either. And there's the dilemma. To live without pain or to live without joy.

They move him gently. His back or neck might be injured and they know to be careful of that, but they cannot leave him face down in the water. They do the best they can and wait for sirens. All are cold, shocked, holding on to themselves, just. Some are silent, others talk occasionally, quietly; one girl is crying, another has her fist pressed to her mouth. Jack is on his side, with as many rugs and bits of clothing as they can find to cover him. They know he is breathing and someone has found a pulse. They keep checking.

It is hard to be sure about a pulse when their own hearts are beating so loud in their ears, and their fingers feel dead. But they are as sure as they can be.

Everyone is very sober now. Tommy stares. He almost cannot move. His face is ashen in the darkness.

Jack must not die. They will not let him.

Jess holds his hand. She pummels it and presses it and wills it to respond. But it doesn't. She talks to him. *Come on, Jack. Come on, Jack. Please.*

Kelly lies a little way off, where she, too, has been pulled from the water. Someone has covered her body with a picnic rug but Jess has already seen it. She had to jump over it as she ran to Jack. A dead body is a strange thing, she discovers. And horrible. Kelly is waxy in her moonlit death. The neck is rather obviously broken. And there is blood. A piece of seaweed is entangled in her hair. Her face is greyer than a human's should be, fish-like, and damp.

All the muscles in Jess's face are tight. Her chest is crushed. She wonders if her head might burst or her heart actually break. She keeps forgetting to breathe. From her mouth comes a strange sound and she realizes that teeth actually do chatter with cold and fear.

The other jet ski has now been ridden carefully onto the beach – bit too late to think about being careful now – and a boy is running towards them all. His face looks terrible.

Jess turns away. She knows it is Simon and she wishes never to see him again or speak to him or anything at all. He should have stayed out of her life and he should stay out now.

She can only think of Jack.

Sirens.

A sob rises in her throat.

Her fingers are crossed. If she prayed, she'd pray. She prays anyway.

If there was a ladder, she'd avoid it.

There isn't.

CHAPTER 44
WAITING

JESS is spinning a coin. Not actually playing Jack's Game yet, because if you're going to play you have to be very sure. Heads or tails, win or lose, life or death: playing the game changes things and you can't escape its rules. Jess knows that now.

She thinks – because she has thought about this quite a lot in the last day and a bit – that if there's a God, He must play Jack's Game. It's not much of an explanation.

Jess is sitting in a horrible waiting room the colour of old white socks. Waiting. The waiting is awful. She needs her guitar, but it wouldn't exactly be appropriate. On the floor is a grubby doll with no clothes and one leg. It lies there with its blue eyes open. It looks shocked, or dead. There is pen scribbled on its stomach and someone has tried to cut its hair. Jess remembers doing that to a doll once.

Jess should be starting a new life now. And perhaps, in a way, she is. For she won't be the same after this, whatever happens.

A flash of anger crosses her mind. She thinks that Kelly... But no, best not to think like that. She is not prone to violent thoughts. But she is in a state of shock, and strange feelings are stirring. She tries to think about anything else.

The bracelet she's wearing. A birthday present from her best friend, Chloe. That was a good day: her mum remembered to rustle up a cake – all the way from Mrs Beaton's Tea Shoppe – and they ate it on the beach, digging their bare heels into the shingle and breathing the seashell air. Her dad phoned and sent the usual money.

But Jess is scared and it's hard to keep her mind on such things as cake, though she must try. And so: it was a fantastic cake; she and her mum used their fingers to scrape the chocolate icing off the wrapping; they have the best cakes in Mrs Beaton's Tea Shoppe.

That Kelly deserved to die? But what does *deserve* have to do with it? The world would be a strange place if everyone got what they deserved.

Keep spinning the coin, Jess. It will help. Focus on the coin. Don't drop it. That's better.

Every time she thinks about Jack, her skin shrinks, goose-bumping. She wants to see him. He's still unconscious and no one knows how long that will be the case, what he'll be like when he wakes. He's lucky to be alive, the doctors say.

His dad is with him now. A nurse said she'd come to the waiting room and get Jess as soon as possible. It's earlier than official visiting hours – she'd slipped out of the house when her mum was still asleep. Left a note, fed Spike. Some things don't change.

Mind you, visiting hours don't really count for patients like Jack. This is a special waiting room. You don't get to be in here if you're waiting for someone with a broken finger.

Jess is trying to make a decision. Does she dare play the game? The sensible part of her knows that she shouldn't. After all, she'd managed to stop Jack taking it so seriously. But Jack's Game *is* serious and perhaps it's all she can do now. Maybe all the spirits and gods and everything else that has a say in the world watch when you play. She is confused and alone and needing him to take the decision away, but when she thinks back to the newspaper stories on his bedroom wall, she knows what *he* would do.

Maybe he was right all along. Maybe there's a risk in *not* doing it. But if so, there's an equal risk in doing it. Jess is more than confused and alone. She is barely holding herself together. If she breathes too hard, she may shatter into a million pieces.

She glances at the clock. Still spinning the coin. With remarkable skill, considering that she's only been practising for two weeks. It almost ripples across her fingers, weaving in and out, a life of its own. Left hand as good as the right. That'll be the piano–playing, and guitar.

Someone comes through the door. A woman. Her eyes are puffy. She grips the hand of a bewildered child with chocolate on its face. Jess doesn't want to look at her, but she's drawn by her grief. She needs to know what it feels like and yet she is afraid of it. The woman picks up the dead doll and gives it to the child, who grins and grabs it by its remaining leg. Jess thinks that if she was the child's mother she'd make her daughter clean and dress it and learn how to love it in more ways than just holding on. The door clunks shut and the air settles again.

Jess rummages in her bag and gets out her iPod, plugs her ear-things in and retreats into her music. Their music. Her senses merge. She closes her eyes, keeps the outside out: the Kelly Gang, the smell, the being really scared. Yesterday. Saturday. Everything. Her mum should be here. Her dad. Someone. A girl shouldn't be here on her own. But then Jess hasn't told anyone she was coming so early, so you can hardly blame them. Her friends were here with her most of yesterday – Chloe, Farah, and others, all in a kind of rota as though they'd worked it out – and Jack's friends – Ella, Chris, Tommy, looking hellish. They all looked hellish. It doesn't matter. It's nothing compared to how they feel inside.

How do they feel? Numb. People say that nothing feels real when something terrible happens. They are wrong. This feels real. It sickens with its reality.

She opens her eyes suddenly, rips out the ear-things. *Breathe slowly, Jess. Almost lost it there. Maybe music is not such a good idea right now. Maybe you should read a magazine, something shallow that won't slice its way deeper than skin.*

Actually, apart from the old sock colour, the room's not that bad. Soft chairs. Free tea and coffee. Plants. A fish tank. They've made an effort, just to stop you thinking. Box of tissues. Cushions. You can't hear sounds from outside, except when the door opens, though there's a buzzing of air-con. It's designed to help you forget where you are. So there's a magazine on sailing and one on houses. And some children's books and toys. She picks up a board book for babies or toddlers or whatever and looks at pictures of diggers and cranes and just does not allow herself to think of what's past that door and what will happen when she is told to walk through it.

Jess is not going to play the game, she decides, suddenly. It would be wrong. It would be falling into the trap of believing it will make a difference. After all, if he hadn't played with luck, or whatever it is, Jack wouldn't be here now.

And yet – it's that word again: *if. If I hadn't done that…* But that's a world that doesn't exist. Might as well imagine waking up as a cockroach – it's that unreal and pointless. So, Jess chooses not to play. She'll never know whether it will make any difference but that is what she must accept.

She continues to let the coin spin through the air though, because it's rhythmical and beautiful, because it takes her mind off everything else, and because she's not thinking. Just playing but not really *playing*.

The door opens. A nurse stands there. Looking at

Jess. If there's a smile, it's an uncertain smile. She's just being friendly, not actually saying anything about Jack. Jess's eyes search the nurse's face, trying to scrape meaning out of what she sees there. She tries to listen to the woman's body language, to read her mind with every sense. It doesn't work.

"You can come and see him now. But don't be shocked when you get in there. It *will* seem shocking at first – everyone's the same. I'll help you – I'll explain everything I can. Come on."

Jess's heart flips. It thumps. Her skin crawls cold. The coin spins through the air and she does not catch it. She stands up, quickly. The coin tumbles towards the ground.

"Don't be scared, love," says the nurse, walking towards her. "I'll be with you."

The coin lands. It rolls. Jess does not look at it. She is not thinking of it. It is nothing. She hurries towards the door, stuffing her iPod into her pocket.

"Is he…? How…?" Her mouth is dry, her voice perforated, the air coming out oddly.

"It's early days, love. But we're hopeful."

Hopeful. Hopeful. *Full of hope.* It doesn't feel like being full of hope. It feels like something so fragile that it cannot be stronger than a thread of smoke.

Jess's knees feel like that too.

Behind her, the coin rolls. Unseen.

Jess walks through the door. The nurse lets her go first.

The coin rolls near the wall. It gently hits the skirting

board at an angle. It wobbles. Stops. Upright, against the wall, wedged in the crevice where the thin carpet slopes slightly.

It stays there. Neither heads nor tails. What do the rules say about that? Jess isn't playing but, playing or not playing, the result will surely be the same.

CHAPTER 45
WIRES AND MACHINES

JESS is rigid as she walks through the glass doors. A small broken sound slips from her lips. The nurse squeezes her arm. Jack's dad looks up, smiles at her. He is holding one of his son's hands.

And everywhere there are tubes. They snake across the body, which is naked from the waist upwards. A bruise spreads from under a dressing. Other dressings patchwork the left side of the torso and that arm is fully bandaged. Bright white tapes spiral around the head and something protrudes from the throat, fixed with more tapes. There is blood, which Jess tries not to look at, and yellow stuff painted on carelessly.

The face is so swollen that she cannot see Jack in it. Bruises pool beneath the eyes.

With rhythmic clunking that seems too slow, a machine pushes air into his lungs through a tube the size of a fat finger. Screens by the bed show green zigzag lines. Jess will not look at them. Something beeps slowly. Between each beep is a silence that is fractionally too long for comfort. You can't not listen to it.

Jess cannot speak. She tries but the right bits are not working. If she speaks she will cry. *Please, Jack, Jack, oh, Jack, wake up.* She so needs him to speak to her. For everything to be as it was before. Before she spun the coin and Jack had to do the forfeit. It would be so simple. She would do something fractionally different – spin it differently, use a different coin, delay him, hold him back with a kiss. He only needed to be in a slightly different place.

It's easy to see the sequence of events that brought him here, the causes. But was there any point at which they could have known in advance? After all, if we can see afterwards that *a* caused *b*, then surely all we needed to do was know or guess that *a* would cause *b* and just stop it happening?

Jack's dad beckons her to sit by him. The nurse finds a chair. Another nurse is doing something, making notes, reading screens. Everything seems very controlled. Jess sits.

The smell of antiseptic comforts her, and yet, something like a mask, it frightens her too.

Jack's dad takes her hand and puts it on Jack's.

"Jess is here," he says to his son. He turns to Jess. His eyes are pink-rimmed and very tired-looking. "Talk to him. He might be able to hear. Hearing's the first sense to come back and we want Jack back now. I know he wants

you here. You can help. By being here, talking to him.
You OK, Jess? Come on, we can do this – we can."

She squeezes Jack's hand. "Hi, Jack. It's me. Jess."
Her voice sounds silly. Jack's dad nods at her.

"Go on, just talk to him. Just about anything. I'm
going to get a coffee. Do you want one?"

Jess shakes her head. She is still looking at Jack's face.
Is he in there? "No, thanks."

Jack. I'm here. It's me. It's Jess.

She swallows. What can she say?

*I hope you're not hurting in there. It looks ...
dramatic. Can you hear me?*

Hey, everyone's thinking of you. Everyone.

*You've got so many cards here. Do you want
me to read them? There's even one from my
mum. Pretty amazing, hey?*

*And this one's from Chris and Ella and Tommy.
Tommy says he's sorry he drank too much.
Didn't make any difference, did it?*

*Jack, I love you. Saturday night was ... so
amazing. I don't know a word for it. I felt so ...
happy. We played brilliantly, didn't we? Do you
remember?*

*I've brought the recording Tommy made. It's on
my iPod. Do you want to hear it?*

Jess looks at the nurse. The nurse is
frowning at the screen. *Can I let him listen?*
The nurse nods.

Floating. Warm. Fuzzy. Nice. Soft. Jess. Jesssssss.

Beep.

I feel her touch. Smile inside. Mouth woolly, not working. Try squeeze. Nothing. Never mind. Later. Jess. Lots time.

Beep.

Floating. Warm. Fuzzy. Nice. Soft. Mmmm.

Smile. Inside. Mouth. Not. Working. At. All.

Jess. Jess. Stay, Jess. I'm. Help. Help!

Beep.

Shiver. Heartbeat. Stuck. Slow. Slow. Sink.

Spinning. That coin where is? I'm spinning, Jess. I'm flying. I see there you down. What doing? Come me with, Jess.

Jess? Jess? Did you spin the coin? Again? Did you? And how did it land? Need to know.

Here. *We can listen to it together. Listen to the cheering, Jack.*

It's my song, the one you liked. I remember the first time I sang it for you. How I felt when you told me it was beautiful. It's all I ever wanted to do, to sing, and singing with you is just the best. You have to get better so we can sing again.

Are you listening, Jack? Can you hear?

Squeeze my hand. Anything. Just, please, just show me. Blink. Or anything. Please, Jack.

I can't...

I need you back. You have to get better. You have to, Jack, please. You have to. Please! Please!

NO! What's happening?

Don't make me go! I'll get his dad.

It's Jack. Something's happening. Hurry!

NO!

Beep.

Any coin, Jess. Doesn't matter. Won't make any. Difference. Real. Was wrong. Or if ... never know. Nothing else. Knowing. Living. Love. Wrong.

Help. Please, Jess, spin it. Can see two paths. One grey, one greyer. Can't choose.

Can't choose. Drifting, Jess. Help. Spinning. Don't ... know ... which ... way ... down. Dizzy. So dizzy. Cold.

So cold.

Can't hear you, Jess. Can't nothing. Dark.

Beeeeeeeeeeeeeeeeeeeeeee

"STAND BACK." *Aaagh.* "AGAIN." *Aaaagh.* "COME ON, JACK!"

Spin.

Beautiful spin. So beautiful.

And now we can only watch as the medical staff try to hurl the life back into Jack's body. It is brutal, battering.

There is nothing to lose now, and yet there is everything. His heart has stopped. It may start again. Or it may not.

The doctors and nurses will do all they can. But in the end it will come down to tiny things that already exist – the state of Jack's being: where his cells are, the precise level of every chemical in his body, the position of every particle, every nano-watt of electricity in his brain, the salts and the ions, the genes and the electrons, the enzymes and the amino acids.

Jack's life is in the balance, such a fragile balance that perhaps simply by watching him we may move a particle.

With Jess and Jack's dad, we watch through the glass door now. We see Jack's poor body being shocked. And listen to him. He is asking us – anyone – to spin a coin, and Jess won't do it, partly because she doesn't know he's asking.

On such a small act of apparent chance does his life now rest.

It's not chance, of course. Jack was right about that. A coin will fall according to how it is spun. Good luck and bad luck are just what we call it.

But there is something else: at this final moment, just when it might be too late, Jack has still not realized the important truth. He is still wrong.

NOTE:

Will you play Jack's Game now? If you're going to play you have to be very sure what you're doing. Heads or tails, win or lose. Even with life and death. That's the rules. Jack's rules.

A life hangs in the balance and either result is equally probable. Heads or tails. Which will it be?

When you are ready, spin the coin – try to spin it beautifully, for this may make a difference; or it may not – and then see which path Jack and Jess's lives will take.

If your coin lands heads up, begin reading on page 278. If it's tails, begin at page 284.

When Oedipus realizes that he has killed his father and married his mother, his mother/wife hangs herself & Oedipus gouges own eyes out. Consequences include countless suicides, murders, curses, famine, plague & a major war. Personally, I blame that interfering prophet – if he'd only kept his mouth shut...

"Thy fate is the common fate of all;
Into each life some rain must fall."
Henry Wadsworth Longfellow
(1807–1882)

"I, at any rate, am convinced that He [God] does not throw dice."
Albert Einstein in a letter to Max Born in 1926.

"A man's character is his fate."
– Heraclitus

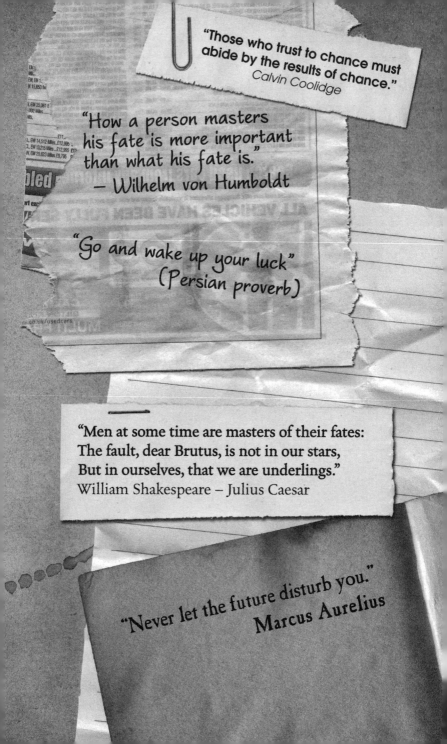

"Those who trust to chance must abide by the results of chance."
Calvin Coolidge

"How a person masters his fate is more important than what his fate is."
— Wilhelm von Humboldt

"Go and wake up your luck"
(Persian proverb)

"Men at some time are masters of their fates:
The fault, dear Brutus, is not in our stars,
But in ourselves, that we are underlings."
William Shakespeare – Julius Caesar

"Never let the future disturb you."
Marcus Aurelius

CHAPTER 46
HEADS

SOME weeks later and August is sinking. A windless, sticky evening. Jess is walking along the beach. It is not easy for her to come here. The memories of that night are still too clear. Her crystal night. They will fade, but she cannot believe that yet.

She had to come here. Often does. Searching for meaning in the air. Thinking. Looking for any sign that it might have been different... Or just needing to be in this place and not being able to stop herself coming. She feels close to Jack here. Jess hugs the memory close. Of Jack wrapping her in his arms on the beach before she spun the coin; of exploring the geography of his knuckles; the smell of him. And how at that moment she could know nothing of what was to come.

The sea is calmer than it was that night. No wind ruffles it; the breakers hiss rather than roar. And the sky is rose-infused. Almost red.

Red. She has thought about red a lot since then. Farantella. Things beginning with "w". How they had laughed about Farantella with her silly prophecies, her nonsense. Because it *was* nonsense. Of course there was something red – if it hadn't been Kelly's top it would have been something else, something red at the prom, anything. She remembers, though she'd not noticed at the time, that Tommy was wearing a red T-shirt. You couldn't go through a day or even an hour without seeing something red. Farantella was safe with that prophecy. And something beginning with "w"? Again, plenty of choice and you can say it was *water* if you really believe that stuff.

Only a fool would make any connection, or someone looking for connections. It is all coincidence. If Farantella had said *blue,* we'd have said it was Jack's jeans, or if she'd said the letter "s" it would have been the *sea* or the *sand* or the *seashell smell* and *smoke* and *sweat.*

But if they had really believed Farantella, it wouldn't have made any difference: Jess knows this, though she cannot exactly explain it. She doesn't know if they could have changed anything, but not knowing is something you just have to deal with. Otherwise it would just be Oedipus all over again. The more she comes here, the more her thoughts clarify: that there was no other way. Too much was out of their control. They could only make small decisions about their present. The future is always another world and meddling with it is dangerous. Just trying to measure it changes it. This is just beginning to make sense. *Or more sense than Schrödinger's cat,* she thinks, remembering how she'd failed to understand the meaning of that.

In her pocket, Jess has petals from Jack's garden, from the roses by the seat where they'd sat together. Where they'd kissed. A choking feeling rises in her throat and she swallows it down.

Leaving her shoes safe on the sand, she walks to the water's edge, churning the surf with her feet. Funny how strong it is, such shallow water. The waves fizz over her shins and knees, stinging, shingly, and gaspingly cold at first.

Jess looks out into the distance. The horizon is clear. No jet skis, no boats. Just endless layers of sky, the waves merging into them. She closes her eyes, takes the petals from her pocket, thrusts her face into them and inhales their scent before throwing them all from her. One or two stick to her hands and she shakes them off. They are carried here and there on wave and air.

Then she takes a coin from her pocket and she throws it with all her strength, as far as she can, and she watches it spiral high, before it arcs down and disappears with no splash that she can see.

Gone.

It's not Jack's coin, of course – that was picked up later by the nurse, who had planned to give it back to Jess, but had then forgotten in the panic of Jack's death. Afterwards, giving it back to the poor boy's girlfriend would have seemed … pointless. No one will ever know which way it would have landed if it had been spun again. The coin Jess throws away now is just any coin, symbolic of all coins. But then Jack's coin was only Jack's *new* coin, nothing special. And what's a coin anyway?

The coin is gone. And Jess is glad. She is angry too, *and* sad, but throwing the coin away is a kind of freedom. If only she had made Jack do that long ago. But then there is no way of knowing what would have been different.

Jess has learnt a truth that Jack never found, with all his philosophy, his cleverness, his intensity, his equilibrium: that fate, like many things, only has power if you believe in it. It is like fairies. Fit for stories. It is to think about but not to live by.

Jess cannot see further than her footsteps home that hot damp evening. She cannot know the things that may or may not happen to her in the rest of her life. But we can guess a little because, looking down, we can see something more than her.

We see her arrive home, tired and red-eyed. Sylvia is sober – she has been ever since Jack and that other girl died. (This may not last but it is a hopeful start. It could be the necessary shock treatment.) Sylvia is needed now; she has a job to do, which may be enough to keep her on the right road. Jess's father, Lorenzo, who will never know how nearly he died himself and how that might have changed things for Jess – for certainly her prom night would have been somewhat different if her father had died a few days before – he is there too; he is staying to help Sylvia till their daughter gets her life back on track. It is kind of him and perhaps unexpected, but actually Lorenzo has discovered, in a difficult conversation with Sam at the funeral, that there is much more to loving his daughter than buying her flowers and champagne and a bracelet. Of course, he is not going to go back to Sylvia, not properly – this is no fairy story and it would do no one any good anyway – but Jess no longer needs to be the thing they fight over. Jess is now something for them to care about together. Until she is ready to move on.

Jess and her mother must look for new roles to grow into. Daughter and mother. They must heal the earthquake crack between them, though perhaps it may have to split a little wider before that can happen.

Death makes you think. It's a beginning.

And there is Spike. Spike spends a lot of time now in Jess's room, curled up into the smell of her. Jess spends much time with her face in Spike's fur. Spike is not fearful and skin-prickly any more and he purrs easily in his cat dreams. When she comes home from her beach walk, he is there at the door with his coiling back and she picks him up. Together they crush the blowsy roses as they brush past and she inhales the scent of them.

Over the weeks and months, they will surely all see Jess begin to live again. To find her own equilibrium. Perhaps she will go to college; perhaps she and Chris, Ella and Tommy will start a band again, find another guitarist. Of course, it won't be the same. But then, nothing ever is.

Chances are that Jess will meet someone else one day. Fall in love again. And that won't be the same either, of course. But it could be just as good. It will depend on many things, like Jess finding a place to keep Jack safely in her memory. This she will do because she is Jess, and strong.

One thing's for certain: she will be changed by her loss. But it will not destroy her: of that we can be confident. She will not be able to sing her song without sadness creeping from the shadows, though this will get less and less until it crushes her no more than a petal might her breath. She will not be able to do many things without thinking of Jack and the smell of him as she buried her face in his neck that night. But she will be happy again soon if she will let herself be. There will come a time when she can touch his picture and smile.

Will she find a way to forgive Kelly? After all, if Kelly could have done things differently, she would have done. Kelly was not properly bad. She was nothing more than a silly, misguided version of the person she might have become if circumstances had been different. If she'd made some different choices or known more or been stronger or different.

So, Jess will live again. Her life will spin like a coin and some things she will have a choice in and others she won't. She has to believe that. Because nothing makes better sense than this: that nothing is until it is and that everything is possible until it isn't.

Jess is beginning to know that.

CHAPTER 47
TAILS

SOME weeks later and August is sinking. A windless, sticky evening. Jess is walking along the beach. It is not easy for her to come here. The memories of that night are still too clear. Her crystal night. They will fade, but she cannot believe that yet.

She had to come here. Often does. Searching for meaning in the air. Thinking. Looking for any sign that it might have been different if only... Or just needing to be in this place and not being able to stop herself coming. Jess hugs the memory close. Of Jack wrapping her in his arms on the beach before she spun the coin; of exploring the geography of his knuckles; the smell of him. It is odd how she needs to come here and find meaning. And how at that moment she knew nothing of what was to come. And how as soon as she starts to wonder *what if I had known*, she cannot make sense of it.

The sea is calmer than it was that night. No wind

ruffles it; the breakers hiss rather than roar. And the sky is rose-infused. Almost red.

Red. She has thought about red a lot since then. Farantella. Things beginning with "w". How they had laughed. Though they don't laugh about it now. About Farantella with her silly prophecies, her nonsense. Because it was nonsense. Of course there was something red – if it hadn't been Kelly's top it would have been something else, something red at the prom, anything. She remembers, though she'd not noticed at the time, that Tommy was wearing a red T-shirt. You couldn't go through a day or even an hour without seeing something red. Farantella was safe with that prophecy. And something beginning with "w"? Again, plenty of choice and you can say it was *water* if you really believe that stuff. And it's really hard not to: But they must try not to. Because that way madness lies.

Only a fool would make any connection, or someone looking for connections. It is all coincidence. If Farantella had said *orange*, we'd have said it was the *fire*, or if she'd said the letter "j" it would have been the *jet skis* or "c" would have been *coin* or "k" would certainly have been *Kelly*.

But if they had believed Farantella, would it have made any difference? Could they have changed anything? Wouldn't it just have been Oedipus all over? They've talked about it since, though not easily. Sometimes these conversations end when Jack becomes very quiet, and touches his head where the scar is visible through his shaven hair. Other times, they seem to move a little further towards a kind of peace.

Leaving her shoes safe on the sand, she walks to the water's edge, her feet churning the surf. Funny how strong it is, such shallow water. The waves fizz over her shins and knees, stinging, shingly, and gaspingly cold at first.

Jess looks out into the distance. She cannot shake off the heaviness. The horizon is clear. No jet skis, no boats. Just endless layers of sky, the waves merging into them. But this time she has come here for a special purpose: she takes a coin from her pocket and she throws it with all her strength, as far as she can, and she watches it spiral high, before it arcs down and disappears with no splash that she can see.

Gone. It should make her feel better but it doesn't.

It's Jack's coin – it had been picked up by the nurse, who had handed it to Jess a couple of days after Jack came round. And Jess had been embarrassed when she took it, almost as if she was being paid for Jack's life.

Jack kept asking about it, though he has begun to ask less now, some six or more weeks later. Jess thinks he is beginning to forget, but he is not. It is still inside him and could eat away at him, if he lets it. Or if she lets him let it.

No one will ever know which way it would have landed if it had been spun again. And although any coin would do just as well, Jess is throwing this one away to symbolize all coins. For what's a coin anyway?

The coin is gone. And Jess is glad. She is angry too, angry that because of a coin they had to go through all this.

She wishes she had made Jack throw it away long ago.

If only.

It could have been so much worse: he could have died, and Jess knows how nearly he did. She cringes inside when she remembers that terrible moment when his heart stopped and they thought it would never start again. Jack feels this too. He cannot say it but there is a blackness where that moment is.

"What was it like?" Jess asked him once, while he was lying in hospital recovering.

"What?"

"Nearly dying."

"I don't remember anything about it."

"What, so no near-death experience? No white light or anything?" She's hoping he'll say no, because she doesn't like the idea that there is a place between something and nothing.

"Nothing. Honestly. Nothing from running into the sea to waking up."

"So, really, we had a worse time than you? And you get all the attention?" She smiles and then she doesn't. "God, Jack, it was just so horrible. I can't tell you."

"Could have been worse. I could have died."

And in his voice is all that knowledge. This is the knowledge that they must leave behind, somewhere in a safe place where it will not hurt them. They must walk away from it without looking back.

"God, you were lucky, Jack."

"I always am."

Jess cannot see further than her footsteps home that hot damp evening. She does not and must not know the things that may or may not happen to her in the rest of her life. But we can guess a little because, looking down, we can see something more than her.

We can see her arrive home. Sylvia is sober – she has been ever since Jack's accident and that girl's death. Jess had screamed at her a couple of days later, something about alcohol and how if it hadn't been for the alcohol in Kelly's blood... And that Jack had seen her drunk and how ashamed Jess had been. Sylvia had cried at that and cried for Kelly and the horror of it. (Jess has not cried for Kelly; there is just a cold place where she was.) Perhaps Sylvia needed to be shouted at and that was what Jess was able to do for her – to shock her into life. Jess's father, Lorenzo, who will never know how nearly he died himself and how that might have changed things for Jess – for certainly her prom night would have been somewhat different if her father had died a few days before – has gone back to the US. Jess had shouted at him too, when he'd said something about missing his lunch-date with her and she'd said, "God's sake, Dad, can't you think of anyone but yourself? Jack nearly died, you know, and all you can think about is lunch?" And then he'd had the usual row with Sylvia. And doesn't it just show that some things don't change? Jess is still the thing they fight over. But in another sense she's not, because she's going travelling, she's getting away, with Jack, as soon as he's fit enough. They're going to India and Thailand and as many dangerous places as they can find.

And Sylvia will not even try to stop them. Somehow, she must find the strength not to. It doesn't matter where she finds that strength from and it doesn't matter if no one ever thanks her – find it she must, for Jess and for herself. In that way, or in some way, they must heal the earthquake crack between them, though perhaps it may have to split a little wider before that can happen. Sylvia will need to find another way to live her life.

Jack and his dad will talk and we must hope that Sam will discover the dark place of guilt that has screwed Jack up. Sam will be horrified to know that this is what his son had felt, after overhearing the conversation with the casserole-bringing woman in the kitchen all those years ago. Oh, and people will bring casseroles while Sam is in and out of hospital with Jack and it may rake it all up for both of them. Tessa will help, of that we can be confident. Friends and all the people who love Jack and Jess and Sam and Sylvia.

And there is Spike. Spike spends a lot of time now in Jess's room, curled up into the smell of her. Jess spends much time with her face in Spike's fur. Spike is sometimes fearful and his skin prickles and in his cat dreams he worries for Jess. One day he may settle but not yet. He senses change and fear. But Spike could be wrong, like Farantella. The prophet who messed up Oedipus's life was doubtless also wrong very often, and it's a shame Oedipus's parents didn't guess that.

Indeed, when Jess comes home from her beach walk, Spike is there at the door with his coiling back and she picks him up. Together they crush the blowsy roses as they brush past and she inhales the scent of them and feels a kind of hope.

One thing's for certain: Jack and Jess will be changed by what has happened. They will be happy again if they will let themselves be and if they make the right choices – if they remember that they can only change the present but the future is another world and not in their control; and if Jess reminds Jack that in the end Oedipus destroyed not only his father and his mother, but himself. And that, in the real world, he would not have had to. If he had only *not* believed in fate.

If we were able to speak to them we could tell them this. Perhaps they could then get on with their lives, controlling their actions as best they can, and understanding that any of those actions could have several results. Nothing is until it is and until then, everything possible is possible.

Luck is just what we call it.

NICOLA MORGAN knew when she left university that she wanted to be a writer. While working to achieve that ambition, she was also an English teacher, and became an expert in literacy and dyslexia. Now, after writing numerous bestselling books for young children, Nicola is the author of many critically acclaimed titles for older children and young adults. Her novels *Fleshmarket* and *Sleepwalking* both won Scottish Art Council prizes, the latter winning the Scottish Children's Book of the Year, and her non-fiction title *Blame My Brain* was shortlisted for the prestigious Aventis Prize.

Nicola lives in Edinburgh but travels widely, visiting schools, conferences and festivals, enjoying any chance to inspire young people about fiction or the workings of their brains.

You can find out more about Nicola and her books at:
www.nicolamorgan.co.uk

Or for Nicola's advice on becoming
a published writer, visit:
www.helpineedapublisher.blogspot.com

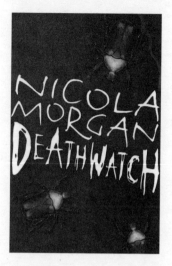

SOMEONE IS WATCHING CAT McPHERSON

BUT SHE IS TOO BUSY TO NOTICE THE SINISTER
EVENTS THAT SHADOW HER.

SPORT IS HER PASSION AND CAT FOCUSES ON HER
TRAINING, NOT REALIZING THAT SHE IS BEING FOLLOWED
BY SOMEONE WITH A REASON TO HATE HER.

WHEN THE STALKER STRIKES,
CAT WILL HAVE TO RUN FOR HER LIFE.

"Edinburgh-based Nicola Morgan uses the capital as a
backdrop for her slick and twisted thriller."
The Scotsman

NICOLA MORGAN

When high-born William de Lacey saves a highwayman's life, he cannot guess how his own life will change. He may have escaped his father's sneering contempt, but has his easy childhood prepared him for the terrifying dangers that he must face now? The stark, ghostly moors are as hostile as the pursuing redcoats, and Will must make some difficult decisions if he is to escape with his life.

NICOLA MORGAN

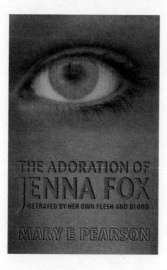

A girl wakes from a coma following a
devastating accident, her memory a blank.
One day she can't walk; the next she can.
One day her right eyelid droops; the next it doesn't.
Her parents call her recovery a miracle –
but at what cost has it come? What are
they hiding from her?

Who *is* Jenna Fox?

"This novel is truly unlike any other I have ever read."
ELLEgirl

**"[An] outstanding examination of identity,
science and ethics."** *Kirkus Reviews*

It's after dark in New York City, and Clary Fray is seeing things. The best-looking guy in the nightclub just stabbed a boy to death – but the victim has vanished into thin air. Her mother has disappeared, and a hideous monster is lurking in her apartment. With her life spiralling into darkness, Clary realizes that she has stumbled into an invisible war between ancient demonic forces and the secretive Shadowhunters – a war in which she has a fateful role to play…

"The Mortal Instruments series is a story world I love to live in." *Stephenie Meyer*